Miracle in a Can

Miracle in a Can

and

Henry the Recycler

C.D. Payne

A i v i a   P r e s s

To: C.P. and N.P.

Warm thanks again to Till Hack and Andy Jacobs for their editorial assistance.

WILDER S. FLINT was driving south on Highway 46 outside Ashtabula, Ohio when he came upon a building shaped like a chicken. The stuccoed exterior had been textured to suggest feathers. Large bird feet, hammered out of tin, extended out on either side of the entry door. A metal sign bolted to the golden beak advertised CHICKEN DINNERS, COMPLETE WITH ALL THE FIX-IN'S for 99 cents. The price originally had been 79 cents, but someone had altered the first digit with a sloppy smear of black paint that had run in streaks down the sign.

Chicken figurines of all shapes and sizes decorated the interior. Boxes of chocolate chickens were for sale by the cash register along with other chicken-themed souvenirs. Wilder sat at the counter; he was the only customer. This could have been a bad omen, except it was nearly three o'clock: well past the busy lunch rush. No waitresses loitered about.

"I'll have the 99-cent chicken dinner," called Wilder to the lone grill man. "And a Coke."

"No chicken on the menu," he replied, scratching a bushy armpit. "I recommend the Hamburger Deluxe."

"Can I see a menu?"

"I recommend the Hamburger Deluxe," he repeated. "Or there's the Cheeseburger Deluxe. But that's a dime extra."

The hamburger tasted like an unknown number of internal organs had been tossed indiscriminately into the grind. The bun was stale. The lettuce leaf gracing the patty bore the imprint of someone's shoe. The greenish and limp French fries had been processed in grease well past its prime. The bottle of Coke was not vigorously chilled. No straw was offered, of course.

The grill man brought out a mug of coffee and sat one stool away from Wilder. He lit a cigarette and played with his lighter. He had a tall pompadour and very hairy arms like he was trying to grow his own sweater.

Wilder smeared extra dollops of mustard on his bun to disguise the taste. He regretted not having splurged on a cheeseburger. The cheese might have offered a distraction from the liverish meat. It was one of the worst burgers he had ever had (certainly ranking in the bottom five), but his mother had raised him to be polite so he didn't complain.

"What year is your Plymouth?" the grill man inquired.

"Thirty-seven."

"I thought so. Looks like the business coupe model. Guess you don't need a back seat."

"It belonged to my uncle," explained Wilder. "He was a sales rep. Dealing in nickel-plated novelties. He carried his sample cases back there."

"He move on to something grander?"

"No. He didn't make it back from the Philippines. Missing in action."

"Guess you were too young for that show. You sorry you missed it?"

"Not at all. I'm in no hurry to get my head blown off."

"Army hasn't drafted you yet, huh?"

"No, but I'm 1A."

"Probably be thrilled to grab a nice strong kid like you. Where you headed?"

"I'm looking for a guy. Ever hear of something called Miracle Creme? It comes in a flat green tin."

"Sure, I got a can of that in the back. Use it to clean my grill. Shines it right up. Got it at the county fair. From one of them demonstrator fellas. You can't buy it in stores. Now I wish I'd bought two. He had the nerve to charge $3 a can, but you could get two for $5. Or five for $10. But who goes to the fair with a spare sawbuck to blow on green mystery goo in a can?"

"What did the fellow look like?"

"Hell if I know. I was watchin' the creme puttin' on its show, not the guy. My wife dips her pin curlers in it and gets a semi-permanent wave."

"Was he good looking?"

"Well, he wasn't ugly or disfigured. I probably would of remembered that. No obvious war injuries."

"How old was he?"

"I don't know. Maybe 25, maybe 30. Not an elderly gent. Had his patter down real smooth. He owe you some money?"

"No, I just want to talk to him."

The bill came to 83 cents. The 17 cents in change Wilder left as a tip. He declined the grill man's offer of a chicken-shaped yo-yo on sale for only 50 cents. He asked the man why there were no chicken dinners to be had in a restaurant shaped like a giant chicken.

"Prices going through the roof," he replied. "Take your breath away what they get for a dressed chicken these days. You know what Truman and his gang are up to don't you?"

"What?"

"They're gut-shanking our money so they can pay off those big war debts with cheaper dollars. And now it's the little guy who has to pay through the nose."

The men's room featured a calendar for the current month (July, 1949) with a redhead lifting up her sweater. Her showcased assets were heavily annotated in pencil and pen by local wags. Wilder took out his fountain pen (a recent high-school graduation gift) and wrote in a neat print across her forehead: "Miracle Creme made me a nympho."

Wilder had to press the starter button three times before his Plymouth rattled to life in a cloud of blue smoke.

He suspected that the five years it sat on blocks in his parents' garage had caused its internals to occlude. Erie High School offered a class in auto mechanics, but scheduling conflicts had consigned him to Spanish instead. He doubted he would ever speak a word of Spanish to anyone, whereas he would always have to worry about keeping a car running. He also suspected that a guy in his likely future income bracket would be facing a long string of aging and temperamental cars.

He did know enough to keep a watch on the oil level in the engine. The spongy pedal also reminded him to refill the brake fluid reservoir every time he bought gas. And something was amiss in the front end, causing the car to wander alarmingly on sharp curves. At least he didn't have to worry about the radio running down the battery. His uncle Paul had been too cheap to buy one. He'd even omitted the optional heater, despite driving thousands of miles every winter across the frozen Midwest.

Uncle Paul won't be feeling the cold now, thought Wilder. His father, however, was not convinced of his brother's demise. He liked to point out that the Philippines consisted of 7,107 islands–any one of which could be harboring his AWOL brother. He claimed to be of the opinion that "lazy ol' Paul" was shacked up with a sarong-draped native on some serene beach. That's why he refused after all these years to turn over the Plymouth keys to Wilder.

When he got his license at age 16, Wilder had agitated for access to the dormant coupe. But his father was not to be moved. "It's not my car to give you," he'd insist. "You'll have to ask your uncle when he returns." His father had paid the yearly registration fee to keep the tags current. He would be handing his brother an itemized bill for those expenses, should he return. So while Wilder rode his bike to school in the snow and ice, enterprising mice built snug winter homes in the becalmed Plymouth. Wilder had cleared out all the nests he could find, but the smell lingered on.

A few miles down the road Wilder stopped for a Negro hitchhiker. He picked up hitchhikers to help him stay awake because he slept poorly these days. The Negro was dressed neatly in a suit and tie. Wilder had thought he might have been a young preacher, but he was a student trying to pay for college by selling magazine subscriptions door to door. He said it was hard work because people could read magazines for free in libraries and some were prejudiced against his race.

Wilder asked him if he liked college. He said it was thrilling because every day he encountered new ideas and new people.

"You don't mind those stuffy professors and all their boring talk?" asked Wilder.

"The secret is to get to know them. Chat them up after class. Get invited to their homes. Baby-sit their kids. Read the books they recommend. If you take an interest, they can really open up. I see you have a fishing pole back there. I can make you a very good deal on a subscription to *Field & Stream*."

"I already get it," lied Wilder.

"I bet your mother would be gratified to receive *Good Housekeeping*. Isn't her birthday coming up?"

"No, it's not."

Wilder steered the conversation around to the green goo in the flat can.

"Miracle Creme, yes, my grandpop uses it to stretch his shoes. A church lady gives him fine Italian loafers that are several sizes too small. He lathers on the creme and sets them out in the sun for a day or two. He says it really relaxes the leather."

"Why does the lady have surplus shoes?"

"She has a spoiled son who is always chasing after the latest styles. Unfortunately, he has rather petite feet. Do you sell that product? Is that why you're on the road in this vintage business coupe?"

"No, I'm just trying to track down the guy who sells it. I hear he makes it in his trailer."

"That could be. I believe my grandpop buys it at a street festival in Columbus."

"Oh, when's that?"

"Uh, September I think."

"Too late. I need to find him right away. As soon as possible."

"How about *Collier's* magazine? It brings a world of fact and fiction to your door every week."

"Sorry, I'm too busy to read magazines."

"I hear that all the time. People are letting their minds go to waste. I'm sure it will be even worse when television takes off."

Wilder, who had never liked school, was of the opinion that most guys went to college to get away from home, get out of the army, and get laid. Not to mention loafing with free eats for four years on daddy's dime or the G.I. Bill. Then there are those graduate students who manage to work the con indefinitely. He was surprised to meet someone who was pursuing his degree for intellectual reasons.

He got to the Trumbull County Fair in Courtland, Ohio around dinner time. The barbecue being offered by vendors smelled enticing, but he made do with a peanut-butter sandwich from his groceries stash in the back of the car. He had cashed in his war bonds for travel money, but had to squeeze every dollar. Gas was alarmingly expensive away from the big towns. He'd been dinged 27 cents a gallon for his last fill-up.

Admission to the fairgrounds was 50 cents, but Wilder

told the gal in the booth he was on army leave and got waved in for free. He went immediately to the exhibition hall, but found no one there selling Miracle Creme. He asked a bald man peddling a patent foam mop if he knew the creme seller, but was abruptly dismissed. He was beginning to suspect these demonstrators were a tight-knit and secretive group. No doubt to protect each other from disgruntled customers demanding refunds.

Fair officials in his experience were just as uncooperative. If you called them to ask if anyone would be selling Miracle Creme at their event, they kept you waiting on hold forever (obliging you to feed quarter after quarter into the pay phone), and then came back to say their vendor lists were strictly confidential. Who did they think he was? Some spy from a competing fair trying to poach away their vendors of the Stick-Forever Fly Paper or the Snore-No-More Dream Pillow?

Feeling dispirited and lost, Wilder wandered about the midway to kill time. Rain had threatened all day, but now the sun had appeared to bathe the tops of the carnival rides in a golden light. He wouldn't have minded an outing on the Tilt-A-Whirl or bumper cars, but such extravagances were out of the question. He did spend a dime on a vast cloud of blue cotton candy because the seller was a cute girl with sandy blonde hair. Done up in a ponytail style that Wilder always found curiously poignant. He figured she was a celebrity cheerleader or majorette back at her high school. He lingered in the vicinity of her stall and made an attempt at conversation.

"You're not very busy," he remarked.

"We do better in the daytime. More little kids then. Don't sell much floss to grown-ups."

"Is this going to turn my tongue blue?"

"Most likely it will," she laughed. "Rot your teeth too."

"I don't see how you can change sugar into this stuff."

"Magic of science."

"Are you traveling from fair to fair?"

"Yup. All summer."

"Sounds like fun."

"Well, it can get to be a grind. Long hours in the heat and humidity. And you're dealing with the public. Some of them can be pretty obnoxious. And I have to keep the flies off the floss."

"I hear some of those fair vendors really clean up."

"Well, you have to pay the fair a percentage of your sales. And there's always the possibility you're a spy for the county making sure all my proceeds go into the till."

"Not very likely. I hear that fellow selling Miracle Creme really does well."

"Yeah, I see lots of folks carrying those cans. I don't think he's at this fair though."

"Too bad. I was hoping to pick up a can. Do you know the guy?"

"Not personally. I seen him around. I hear he's very nice."

"What's his name?"

"Why do you want to know that?"

"Just curious. Uh, I was wondering if he might need some help."

"Sorry, I got to spin some more stock now. Nice talking to you."

Wilder thought about calling his parents and felt guilty when he decided not to. His father was out on strike at the screen-door plant and he didn't want to hear any updates on that mess. His mother would want him to come home Right Now. They would be Disappointed in him and regard his actions of the past week as Very Immature. Why spend a dollar or more on that conversation when he could have it for free in his head?

He slept that night in the Plymouth where it was parked in the fair's grassy lot. Lying on the diagonal on the thin plywood that substituted for a back seat and extending his legs into the trunk he could recline nearly full length. (Uncle Paul had broken a dozen hacksaw blades laboriously sawing out the steel panel that originally divided the trunk from the car interior.) The spare tire and his grip Wilder moved to the front seat. Even with all the windows closed mosquitoes found their way in and gave him hell. They buzzed by his ear before biting him leisurely so as to prolong the torture. He decided he would have to find one of those military surplus stores and buy an air mattress and a can of DEET.

He crawled out of the car at dawn and showered with a couple of early-rising carnies in a tent that was missing its back wall. A large rusty propane tank supplied the gas boiler that heated the water. Wooden pallets elevated the bathers above the soapy puddles. A group of giggling high-school girls on their way to a barn to groom their sheep for that day's competition made a point of veering off course to stroll behind the tent. Startled, Wilder kept his back to them, but the carnies weren't so modest.

After dressing hastily, Wilder decided to chance a stab at breakfast in the carnival's cook tent. He was loading up a paper plate when a fat man in a greasy visor cap said, "Who the hell are you?"

"I'm Ed," Wilder replied. "I got hired on last night."

"By who?" he demanded.

"I didn't catch his name. A big guy. Sunburned and missing some teeth."

"I wish to hell Lyle would inform me of these matters. See me at the office trailer as soon as you're done. And I mean pronto."

Wilder gulped down his breakfast, then refilled the plate and filled his thermos from the coffee urn. He hurried out to his car with his bounty. After the usual anxious moments with the Plymouth's aggrieved starter, he drove down the road and pulled in behind a billboard so he could finish his breakfast in peace. Sipping his coffee, he consulted his notebook and fold-out road map. He could head to the county fair in Springfield or return to Pennsylvania and try his luck in Jefferson Township. His special quarter came up heads, so Ohio it was. It was one of those coins painted with red nail polish so the management of a place with a jukebox could feed it into the slot and not count it as income when they emptied the box. It had escaped into the wild and now occupied a reserved spot in Wilder's pocket.

The Ohio map was dense with roads, but only some of them were hard-surfaced. A driver who valued his time and shocks had to choose his route carefully. Wilder decided to head south and pick up Highway 62 outside Alliance. It was all new territory to him. He stuck to the posted speed limits, especially in the small towns where he figured his Pennsylvania plates made him a choice target for tickets. As far as he was concerned the entire Buckeye state was one big speed trap.

After a string of silent hitchhikers, Wilder picked up a man in Canton who was on his way to check out a Studebaker in a junk yard in Beach City.

"I think it might be my car that was stolen," he said. "Repainted, of course, and then wrecked."

"Have you checked with the cops?" Wilder asked.

"I make it a habit to steer clear of the cops."

"Do you want the car back?"

"Depends on how badly it's damaged. And, frankly, I wouldn't mind seeing some blood stains on the seats."

"Car thieves are the lowest of the low," affirmed Wilder, who technically had not received permission to be piloting the Plymouth. In fact, knowing his father, it was not inconceivable that it had been reported as stolen despite the note he'd left on the dining-room table next to the bowl of wax fruit. He prayed his mother had intervened to squelch that call. Still, it was possible he could be pulled over at any moment by the long arm of the law.

The man offered Wilder a Camel cigarette, but he declined. He figured he worked too hard for his money to affix a lifelong nicotine leach to his wallet. The man lit his coffin nail with the Plymouth's lighter; Wilder hoped his anemic battery could handle the amperage draw.

As the man had no experience with Miracle Creme, the conversation turned to unfaithful girlfriends. He said he'd been freezing his ass off in Belgium in the winter of 1944 and waiting for the next mortar round to put him out of his misery when he got a "Dear John" letter from his girl.

"She ditched me for a metallurgist at a steel plant in Youngstown. He had one of those deferred occupations. Vital to the war effort you know."

"Yeah, and probably making out like a bandit from all the overtime."

"I expect he was salaried. Those positions usually are. My sister went to their wedding. The girl was a friend of my sister, you see. That's how I met her. My sister introduced us."

"Still your sister could have boycotted the function out of loyalty to you."

"Yeah, I felt the same way at the time. Well, it's all water over the dam now."

"I don't suppose you ever see her."

"The girl? I see her once a year. On Halloween."

"How's that? You go to the same party?"

"No. I know where she lives in Youngstown. I drive there and park my car around the block. I put on a mask. Then when a group of trick-or-treaters go up to her door,

I hang back like I'm one of the dads. I watch her hand out the candy."

"You do that every year?"

"So far I have. Sometimes I take along an extra mask so I can see her twice."

"And she never notices you?"

"So far she hasn't. Not anyway that she's let on."

"How does she look?"

"She looks good. Does her hair differently now. Same lipstick though. Always the reddest red you've ever seen. That's what I first noticed about her. Anyway, she looks happy. I expect she's happier with him then she would have been with me. No kids yet that I've seen. If she has a baby, I'll probably stop going."

"Right. Does your sister still talk to her?"

"I don't know. I don't have anything to do with my sister any more."

"You think you'll get another car before next Halloween?"

"Oh, I have a car. It's parked in my garage. A red Merc convertible. Bought it new last year."

"Why aren't you driving it?"

"Judge yanked my license. Too many tickets."

"You got a heavy foot, huh?"

"No, I have a tendency to drink to excess. Mostly at night. Rye whiskey. I developed a taste for it in the Army. I'm OK during the day. The hangovers I can manage. I suggested to the judge he only withdraw my right to drive at night. So he tacked on another $50 to my fine for being facetious. It doesn't pay to open your mouth in court."

The man flicked his butt out the open window.

"Beach City is a mile or so down the road. You can let me out there."

Since the man seemed knowledgeable about cars, Wilder asked him if he thought the Plymouth was good for any extended trips.

"Well, I don't hear any rod knocks or bearing rumbles, so your motor's probably OK for a while. If you pull any long grades you'll want to stop at any sign of overheating. Your front end is your big problem, bud. It feels like it's totally shot. Does it shimmy?"

"Not if I keep my speed under 50."

"This car really isn't safe to drive in its present condition. You probably shouldn't be subjecting passengers to these unnecessary risks. But I do thank you for the lift."

When he pulled over to let the man out, he insisted on paying Wilder $2 for gas.

"Take it, kid," he said. "You need it more than I do. I hope you find what you're looking for. And get those kingpins looked at."

"Thanks. I hope your Studebaker's worth salvaging."

"Oh, I expect it's a wreck. I'm probably just down here to satisfy my ghoulish curiosity."

Wilder spent his unexpected windfall on a Chinese dinner in a suburb of Columbus. His father was always pointing out newspaper articles about unwary diners contracting ptomaine poisoning in chop-suey joints, but Wilder favored oriental cuisine, finding it both tasty and cheap. His very first date had climaxed with the three-course dinner for two at Erie's most authentic Chinese restaurant. They had seen an Ida Lupino movie and had a very garlicky make-out session later in her parents' driveway.

The Columbus waitress was wearing a slinky Chinese-style dress even though she was a middle-aged white woman. Wilder wondered if the plastic flower in her hair was a compulsory part of her uniform. He asked her if she had ever heard of Miracle Creme in a can.

"Oh, yes, I used to rub it on my kids' gums when they were teething. Settled them right down."

"You mean it's not poisonous?"

"Heavens no. I had to hide the tin so my kids wouldn't smear it on their toast. They preferred it to butter. A tablespoon or two adds a real zest to meatloaf. Too bad you can't find it in stores. I buy it at a street festival."

"The one in September?"

"That's right, honey. I wouldn't miss it for the world!"

The paper slip in his cookie read: "Seek kindness first and beauty last."

Not Wilder's idea of a fortune. He preferred the kind that said he would obtain great wealth and be admired by millions.

Out in the parking lot a girl came up to him and asked if he was headed west. She was wearing what looked like a man's Stetson hat and had a half-filled Navy duffel bag slung over her shoulder. She was dressed in blue jeans with rolled-up cuffs, embroidered slippers, and a man's brown rayon shirt with tan piping outlining the collar and two chest pockets.

"I'm only going as far as Springfield," he replied.

"What direction is that?"

"Due west according to my map."

"May I hitch a ride with you?"

"Well, I don't know. I've been advised my car is not safe for passengers."

"It's probably safer than my loitering on this street corner after dark."

"All right, I guess so. It's the old Plymouth over there."

"Too bad. I hoped you were driving that big shiny Lincoln."

"What's that smell?" she exclaimed when they were underway.

"This car was out of commission for a few years. Some mice moved in."

"I hope they've all moved out."

"Yeah, I hope so too."

"And it looks like they made off with your back seat."

He explained the concept of Detroit's business coupe.

"So where are you going?" asked Wilder.

"San Francisco."

"Really? You think it's safe for a girl to hitchhike that far?"

"I can take care of myself."

"I guess it's good that you're kind of skinny."

"Thank you for informing me that I'm not attractive."

"That's not what I meant."

"That's exactly what you meant. Well, you're no Tyrone Power yourself."

"I just meant that San Francisco is a long way off, and girls traveling alone can be the target of unsavory characters. You should be careful whose car you get into."

"Too late. I'm already in yours."

"Why are you going to Frisco?"

"Why? Because it's a cultured and cosmopolitan city."

"I mean what are you going to do there?"

"I intend to immerse myself in the Bay Area milieu."

"Is that a river or something?"

"Oh my, you are the village rustic. Or was that an attempt at drollery? I suspect not. What remote pocket of the Keystone State are you from, Tyrone?"

"You noticed my license plate, huh? I'm from Erie."

"Was it eerie growing up in Erie?"

"Only in the winter when the wind blows in off the lake and the snow piles up to the rooftops."

"Sounds like a living nightmare. I'm from New York."

"State or city?"

"Let's get one thing clear, Tyrone. When someone says they're from New York, they're talking about the city. Although I suppose they could be from Brooklyn, the Bronx, or even–God forbid–from Queens. People with an intention to deceive might say they're from New York when in fact they live in New Jersey. And then there are the real phonies like me who are actually from Connecticut."

"Where? Hartford?"

"God, no. I'm from Greenwich. That's right across the border. My father works in Manhattan so I am by proximity a New Yorker."

"What does he do?"

"He works in advertising. He gets his clients mentioned on the radio."

"Like who? Al Capone?"

"Hardly. Say you have a radio drama where a character says, 'I'm meeting Ethel for lunch downtown.' My father works his magic and now the character says, 'I'm meeting Ethel for lunch at Howard Johnson's.'"

"And does her friend then say, 'Be sure to look for the familiar orange roof'?"

"That would be too blatant. They try for a measure of subtlety. It's a commercial plug, but it should sound integral to the story. Slipped discreetly into the listeners' minds, as it were. Yet within two days all the Howard Johnson's in areas where the program was aired will report a slight uptick in business. What does your father do?"

"He's a shift supervisor at a screen-door factory, but he's out on strike."

"Really? If he's a supervisor, isn't he part of management?"

"That's what the company thinks, but my dad isn't buying it."

"How much does he make?"

"$82.50 a week."

"God, I'd be out on strike too. Does he know you're off barreling through Ohio in this antique automobile?"

"I left them a note. Do your parents know where you are?"

"I did the note thing too."

"Where did you sleep last night?"

"Oh, one track mind, huh? I slept at the Columbus YWCA. You would have liked it. Six girls to a room and all in various stages of undress."

"How much did they clip you for that?"

"$1.45."

"Well that's reasonable."

"And where did you pass the night, Tyrone?"

"In the back of my car. That reminds me. Keep your eyes peeled for an army surplus store."

"Why? Do you intend to buy a bayonet and eviscerate me?"

"I need an air mattress and some mosquito repellent."

"I have a bottle of that in my duffel. The insects in this state are brutal. Now I see why the cognoscenti rarely venture west of the Hudson."

"Who are they?"

"Believe me, you've never met one. And why are you being drawn like a moth to the flame to Springfield, Ohio?"

"I'm going to a fair there."

"Are you hoping to have an affair there at the fair?"

"No, I'm looking for a fellow."

"Who?"

"Just a guy I need to discuss something with."

"Oh, a man of mystery, huh? I fear you are harboring some dark secrets, Tyrone."

"My name's Wilder. Wilder Flint."

"You're kidding."

"No. That's my name. Wilder S. Flint. What's yours?"

"Verity. Verity Warren."

"Doesn't Verity mean something?"

"It means truth. Perhaps intended ironically since my father works in advertising. It derives from the Latin, although no one speaks that dead language. Perhaps my parents hoped I'd grow up and marry the Pope."

"I don't think he dates much."

"Too bad. Those Italian girls have curves like nobody else, including me, alas. But you've already pointed that out."

"Sorry. No offence intended."

"But much taken, Wilder S. Flint. Much taken. I suppose you got teased mercilessly for that screwball name."

"Pretty much non-stop. Did you get teased for your name?"

"Certainly not. I have a perfectly normal and acceptable name. You should see my signature. It really is a work of art. The subsequent W echoes and multiplies the dramatic strokes of the V. I suppose your signature is a crude and illegible scrawl."

"It's OK. I never gave it much thought. My middle name is Samuel in case you're interested."

"Kind of an anti-climax after Wilder, don't you think? But preparing you for the cruel disappointment of Flint."

"What's wrong with Flint?"

"Nothing at all. I'm sure the Indians appreciated it for starting their campfires. And how would a Zippo light your cigar without it?"

They drove on in silence for a few miles.

"They make Zippo lighters in my home state," Wilder said. "In Bradford. That's a ways east from Erie. I'd like to take their factory tour someday."

"A man with a dream. I like that. Yet you don't own a Zippo yourself."

"How did you know that?"

"I'm remarkably observant. You give off no tobacco aromas. No nicotine breath. Nor is there the telltale outline of a

Zippo showing in any of your pockets. I said to myself here is a fellow with no bad habits. A good-looking guy devoting himself to clean living. A man who will haul you down the road without imperiling your honor."

"Well, it's true. I don't smoke."

"You could still tote a Zippo, you know."

"To do what?"

"To be a gentleman and light other people's cigarettes. To signal passing airplanes if you're lost in the woods. To light the way if you're pursuing someone down dark alleys. To signal a fellow conspirator if you're spying for Russia. To explore an Egyptian tomb. To light candles for a romantic dinner for two."

"I could, but I expect it would just sit in a drawer. A match works just as well most times. The Zippo and the zipper are both products of Pennsylvania. That's a fact your average person is not aware of."

"The zipper too, huh?" she said, briefly eyeing his crotch.

"They make those down in Meadville. The Depression skipped that town because everyone was so busy making zippers. They cranked out a quarter-million miles of zippers for the war effort."

"So Hitler didn't get zapped. He got zipped."

"He committed suicide in his bunker. He should have done that in 1933 and saved everyone a lot of bother."

They made good time to Springfield on U.S. 40, a major four-lane road. Wilder stayed over in the right-hand lane with the trucks and other aging pre-war cars. He offered to let Verity out in downtown Springfield, but she said she would never forgive herself if she didn't experience a genuine Midwestern county fair.

The fair was much larger than the previous day's. One sign of its higher aspirations was the youth with a 4H badge and clipboard in the lot collecting a dollar from each car for parking.

"I hope this fee also gets us into the fair," said Wilder, reluctantly forking over his buck.

"Sorry, you gotta pay at the gate too," replied the boy.

"I wonder how many of those dollars are going into that kid's pocket," said Verity.

"Probably plenty if he's smart. I need to get me one of those clipboards."

Wilder tried his soldier-on-leave ploy again at the gate.

"What regiment are you with?" demanded the booth agent.

"Uh, uh," stammered Wilder.

"That'll be one dollar for two adult admissions," said the man.

Wilder meekly paid and they shuffled through the turnstile.

"Some soldier boy you are," commented Verity.

"It's worked in the past. The dude caught me by surprise. Next time I'll say the 82nd Airborne."

Verity was all for heading to the midway, but Wilder steered her toward the commercial hall. They went up and down the rows at a rapid pace.

"Look at all this crap," she said. "Who buys this junk? And why would I need to cut small circular holes in glass?"

"Be handy if you were a burglar. That's a pretty snazzy tool."

Since the guy cutting all the glass into spirals and ribbons seemed friendly, Wilder asked him if he could point them toward the Miracle Creme booth.

"I don't think Boyd's at this fair. Least ways I haven't seen him."

"You know where he might be then?"

"Couldn't really say."

"What's Boyd's last name?"

"Why do you want to know that?"

"I owe him some money. I want to write him a check."

"Sorry. I got a business to run here. You're blocking my show. Buy something or move on, kid."

At Verity's insistence they stopped at a nearby booth to get Wilder a pair of 79-cent aviator sunglasses.

"Why do I need these?" he asked. "I don't mind the sun."

"You'll thank me in 50 years when your eyes aren't shot through with cataracts."

Wilder stuck his selected pair on his nose. "There. Are you satisfied? Do I look like Gregory Peck in 'Twelve O'clock High?'"

"You look more like the blind man selling pencils on the corner. No, you look good. Like they're gassing up your B-25 for another run over Tokyo. How tall are you anyway?"

"I'm six-one if I don't slouch."

"Does your mother tell you not to slouch?"

"Yeah, she's been known to."

They went to look at the livestock pavilions; Verity was impressed.

"Look at that pig, Wilder. It's immense. It's nearly as big as your car. I had no idea pigs reached that size. You could stick armored spikes on its back and pass it off as a dinosaur. I bet it could feed a family of six for a year, assuming they weren't Jewish. What part do they get the bacon from?"

"I have no idea."

"Don't be so gloomy, Wilder. What's with your Miracle Creme fixation? It sounds like something my mother would be obsessing over. If it's sold in a swanky jar, costs a fortune, and is reputed to have anti-wrinkle properties, I'm sure my mother would order it by the case."

"It's a personal matter, Verity. I'm not really interested in

Miracle Creme. In fact, I wish I never heard of the stuff. I just want to locate the guy who sells it."

"And why is that?"

"I told you. It's a personal matter."

"Do you intend to do him bodily harm? Are you carrying a gun?"

"No to both questions. Jesus, what do you take me for? And shouldn't you be heading off to the nearest YWCA?"

"Not likely, Wilder," she said, taking his arm. "We haven't ridden any rides yet."

The sun had set and the midway was ablaze with swirling colored lights.

"This isn't a date," Wilder pointed out. "I don't really know you. I expect we'll be parting shortly. I don't really have the funds to be buying anyone tickets on carnival rides."

"Gee, Wilder, you really know how to make a girl feel special. OK, I'll buy us both a ride on the Ferris wheel. I hope you don't mind sharing a seat with me."

"That's fine, Verity. I have no objection to you personally. I just don't want to run out of money this far from home. You'll recall my father's out on strike. He can't be wiring me any emergency money."

"Right. And even when he's working he only makes $82.50 a week."

"Well, they're aiming to get a raise if the strike is successful."

"I can tell you one thing, Wilder. I'm not buying any screen doors until that strike is settled."

"Glad to hear it. We thank you for your solidarity."

The wheel wasn't as big as the one at Hershey Park, but they still oohed and ahhed at the grand vista spread out before them at the top. Wilder held Verity's hand because that was the expected etiquette on carnival rides. It was a slimmer hand than another he had held in the recent past. He felt he should make an effort at conversation as they rotated about.

"Your father being in the radio game, Verity, I suppose he knows those big stars like Bing Crosby, Fred Allen, and Eddie Cantor."

"Well, he's met them, of course, but they're not exactly bosom pals. I mean they're not in constant communication trading horse-racing tips. They don't swap dirty stories in the steam room while lounging in the nude. He has played golf a few times with Al Jolson."

"Al Jolson. That's impressive. How about Dick Powell?"

"What about him?"

"Isn't he married to Ruby Keeler?"

"No, that was Al Jolson, but they got divorced. Dick Powell was married to Joan Blondell but now he's married to June Allyson. Personally, I would have stuck with spunky Joan. The names are so similar I bet he gets them confused at times. Your wives probably won't have that trouble unless they next marry a Wheldrake or a Waldorf."

"I expect my wife will want to stick with me for good."

"Every guy thinks that, bub. Until the sex goes south after six months."

"My parents have been married for 27 years. They seem quite compatible."

"Did you say compatible or contemptible?"

"You know what I said."

"Just teasing you, Wilder. You have a personality that invites teasing."

"I don't imagine you know much about my personality, having just met me this evening."

"You'd be surprised what I knew about you–after the first five minutes."

Feeling guilty about being an avowed cheapskate, Wilder bought his date a banana split funnel cake. It was such a large concoction, he had to help her finish it. Then he asked a few more carnival workers about Boyd, the Miracle Creme man, but got no useful information.

Back at the car Wilder asked if she had the address of the Springfield YWCA.

"I doubt if they would be of much help, Wilder. They only have the residential halls in big cities."

"It's after eleven. Where do you intend to sleep?"

"Where are you sleeping?"

"Right here in my car. Assuming they don't kick us out. That's why I parked out here at the back of the lot."

"Oh, I wondered about that. I thought you were afraid someone was going to dent your nice car. How about I sleep in the back and you take the front seat?"

"Sorry, I have to decline that offer. Not being a midget."

"OK, can I bunk in your front seat?"

"I suppose. If you want. But it's not going to be very comfortable."

"Yeah, I'm anticipating that. I accept your proposal with the understanding that you will be a gentleman and keep your hands to yourself."

"Of course. That goes without saying."

"Fine, but you don't have to sound so resolute. I hope I'm not completely unattractive."

"You're a very nice girl, Verity. And not bad looking. I'd like you as a friend, assuming we had known each other longer."

"That's a rather convoluted thought, Wilder. I'll have to parse it later for deeper meanings."

"Fine by me. Let's break out that mosquito repellent of yours. I'm getting eaten alive out here."

Much rearranging was required since Verity was bedding down where normally at night Wilder stowed his spare tire, grip, and fishing pole. Plus, her duffel was not as small as it first appeared. Eventually, everything and everyone got sorted out. Wilder immediately regretted that he hadn't made purchasing an air mattress his top priority for that day. Nor was it easy to fall asleep with his roommate violently shaking the car as she struggled to comport her slim body in the constricted space provided by Mr. Chrysler's engineers. Plymouth was, after all, his low-priced brand. Motorists who wished to sleep in their cars in comfort could go to Nash and buy its deluxe model with seats that folded down to make a bed.

In time the sounds of the fair faded away, a mist rose from the damp earth, the eastern sky beyond the line of maple trees brightened, and birds began to sing their morning song.

Chapter 2

Bony promontories of his hips and shoulders, throbbing acutely, crossed a threshold of pain that jolted Wilder awake. He opened his eyes. Above him loomed an upside-down face surmounted by a Stetson. His companion was observing him from the front seat. She had taken the time to freshen her lipstick.

"Sleeping Beauty awakes," she said.

"Not willingly," he groaned. "I'm only awake because my body hurts."

"Hah! You should talk. I feel like I spent the night digging a new Erie Canal–through solid granite. It's enough to make a girl long for her cozy suburban bedroom."

"You should forget this transcontinental nonsense and go back home."

"I wouldn't give them the satisfaction."

"Where did you get that hat?"

"Off a truck driver in Jersey who tried to get fresh. He came out much the worse for wear. I'm still waiting for you to compliment it."

"You look like James Cagney's kid sister."

"Thanks. Your eyes are much bluer in the morning, Wilder, than they are at night."

"I doubt that."

"Just a little mascara to darken your eyelashes and the effect would be quite sensational."

"Here's a news flash, Verity. Guys don't wear make-up."

"They do out in Hollywood."

"Could be, but not in real life. You need to button some of those buttons."

"You're kind of a prude, Wilder S. Flint," she replied, buttoning up her shirt. "I should point out this butch ensemble is not my usual style. It was purchased specially for the road to inhibit the male sex drive. I can see it's working with you. The boyish look was inspired by Katherine Hepburn's wardrobe in 'Sylvia Scarlett.' When I reach the western plains, I'll be donning cowgirl duds modeled on Paulette Goddard's fanciful dude-ranch apparel in 'The Women.'"

"Sorry, I didn't see those movies."

"Frankly, that doesn't surprise me. Oh, I've made another interesting discovery."

"What?"

"I found a notebook under the seat. Inside was this curious letter."

"Hey, give me that letter! It's rude to snoop through people's private stuff."

"I'm just protecting myself. That notebook might have contained your diagrams for my planned vivisection."

"I wish it did."

"Shall I read the letter?"

"Please don't."

"OK, here goes: 'Dear Mom and Dad, I got a job with the man who sells Miracle Creme. I should be back home before Christmas. Please don't worry. Love, Dot. P.S. I won't be that far away. His route is mostly through Ohio.'"

"You shouldn't read people's private letters."

"What about you? I see no evidence this note was addressed to you. Are you the dad in question? Has your daughter run away with the Miracle Creme man?"

"You don't know anything about it."

"At first I thought perhaps these mystery parents had

commissioned you to find their missing daughter. Then I decided no, you were much too personally involved. Then I thought maybe she was your sister. Except in all the time I've known you, you've never once mentioned having a sister."

"It's none of your business."

"By the way, I've got three brothers. Two older, one younger. Did I mention that?"

"I'm sure I couldn't care less."

"Then it hit me. This absconding Dot person is your *girlfriend!* Or should I say your ex-girlfriend?"

"What if she is? What business is it of yours?"

"I think it's time you got this off your chest, Wilder. It's time for you to come clean."

"I'm hungry, Verity. Let's go back to town and find a diner. I'll tell you all about it and then I'll drop you off on Highway 40. You can stick out your thumb and get a lift from some deranged fruitcake."

"Two in as many days. That's not very likely."

The diner on Main Street was named The Cave. Its interior was decorated with large fake rocks and papier-mâché stalactites. The Formica on the counter simulated freshly blasted rock. The napkin and sugar dispensers appeared poised to tip into deep crevices. Wilder ordered the Subterranean 3-Egg Special, Verity had the Mine Shaft Pancakes with a side of Boulder Bacon.

"OK, Wilder dear, let's have it," she said. "And please start from the beginning."

"Oh, all right. I'm 1A. Do you know what that means?"

"Sure. You're all set to go toe-to-toe with big Joe Stalin."

"That's right. The U.S. Army has a mortgage on my hide. And they'll be calling it in any day now."

"You could get deferred by going to college."

"I hate school. Always have, always will. So it was my dad's idea for me to go to welding school."

"I thought you hated school."

"I do, but he said trade school would be different. He said in ten weeks that school could teach me a valuable trade. He said a skilled welder can always get a good job anywhere. He said the Army would be impressed by my welding diploma and might train me to be a machinist. I wouldn't just be a grunt in a foxhole."

"You want to be a machinist?"

"Hell, I don't know. Probably not. So I spent half my savings signing up for this welding school in New Philadelphia. My dad saw their ad in the back of a magazine. Classes there started two days after I finished high school."

"Where's New Philadelphia? Is it near the old Philadelphia?"

"No, it's in Ohio. South of Canton a ways. Anyway I go there and discover that welding is about the most boring occupation on earth. You have to coax along this little puddle of molten metal and hope the torch doesn't set you on fire."

"Looks like welding is out as your career."

"It's like those farmers in North Dakota plowing 10,000 acres of wheat fields. There's not enough going on to keep the mind alive."

"It does sound rather tedious. Think of all those Liberty ships they had to weld up during the war. Miles and miles of welds in each ship. The mind boggles."

"Right. A lot of those shipyard welders were girls, who I guess were just happy to have a job. Or maybe they had way more patience than me. But I couldn't leave welding school because that would disappoint my dad, who's got my whole future all figured out. And I couldn't marry Dolores because the Army is going to draft my ass."

"Wait, your girlfriend is named Dolores? Then who's this Dot person?"

"Dot is her nickname."

"No, Dot is the nickname for a girl named Dorothy."

"Well, I've known Dolores since she was four and people have always called her Dot."

"Pennsylvania is even more backward than I imagined. Why did you want to marry this faux Dot?"

"Why? Why does anyone want to get married? Because I love her. I've been going steady with her all my life."

"No, only since you were four."

"Still, that's a long time."

"Were you engaged? Was she exhibiting your microscopic diamond on her ring finger?"

"No, because I'm 1A. We couldn't make any plans. My life would be different if I had flat feet or a heart murmur."

"Or leprosy, that might work. Or if you were hideously and grotesquely deformed."

"The point is if I was unfit to serve, I might be married already. So there I am being miserable and lonely in New Philadelphia, and I get a phone call from Dot's upset mother."

"Right. Your so-called sweetheart had blown town. Did she leave you a note?"

"Nothing. I haven't heard from her at all. Not one word."

"Wow, that's harsh. Did you have an argument?"

"Not at all. We always got along great."

"Did you sleep with her and prove to be a dud in bed?"

"She's not that kind of girl, Verity. She's saving herself for marriage."

"Or for some stud named Boyd. What are their traveling arrangements?"

"I talked to a watchman at the fairgrounds back home.

He said the guy has a pretty fancy trailer. One of those new Spartans. All riveted aluminum like a B-29. He tows it with a Cadillac."

"I doubt that trailer has two bedrooms, Wilder."

"She might be bedding down on the dinette. They usually make into a bed."

"Right. And Boyd might have a war injury rendering him harmless in that department. But I doubt it."

"You think she's sleeping with him, huh?"

"This isn't a movie, Wilder. This isn't a script being written for the Catholic Legion of Decency starring Shirley Temple as a doe-eyed bobby-soxer. Girls have sex with guys. They do it all the time."

"Then why wasn't she having sex with me?"

The waitress, dressed in a pink hard hat to match her uniform, sidled closer to hear the reply.

Wilder examined the check.

"Let's pay the bill and go. Your share is, uh, 70 cents."

"That could be your problem, Wilder. Your dates with Dot, did you always go dutch?"

"Never. But you're not my date."

Wilder paid the bill and asked the waitress for a phone book.

"Who you looking for, hon'?" she said. "I know most everyone in town."

"An army surplus store."

"That would be Max's Discount, corner of Light Street and Victory Highway."

"Where's the Victory Highway?"

"That would be U.S. 40; it's our main drag. I hope you find your girlfriend. I just love Miracle Creme. I mix a little in my husband's farina, and he's a real dynamo in bed. You might try some if you're having trouble in that department."

"Don't tell him that," said Verity, helping herself to a minty toothpick. "He's all over me day and night as it is."

Outside Max's Discount store on busy Highway 40 Wilder shook Verity's hand and wished her well.

"Send me a postcard from Frisco. Assuming you make it there without being dismembered by some lunatic."

"Save your bon voyages, Wilder. I'm coming with you."

"You're what?"

"Hey, I need to know how this saga turns out. Don't worry. I'll stay out of your hair. I might even chip in a little for gas. And I'm a much better map reader and navigator than you are."

"And where are you going to sleep?"

"We'll get two air mattresses. Your car's all-business back pit is big enough for two."

"I doubt that. Besides, what would people think?"

"Here's a news flash, honey. The only person we know in this state is that nosy waitress back at Cave City. And she already thinks we're sleeping together."

"Yeah, thanks to your big mouth. And what do I say to Dot when I show up with some girl?"

"You tell the truth. You say I'm a hitchhiker who wanted to see the fair. Or if she's shacked up with hunky Boyd, you introduce me as your fianceé just to watch her burn. Girls never like to see a guy they've ditched wind up with something better."

"Dolores is a very lovely and charming girl."

"Meaning what exactly?"

"Never mind. All right, we'll give it a try. But remember I'm not interested in any girl except Dot. And I reserve the right to dump you out on the road if it doesn't work out."

"Sure. That's fair."

"And you know my car is unsafe. We could both die in a fiery crash."

"That's much less likely to happen with me in the seat beside you. It makes for a more balanced load."

"I'm sure that's total bunk, but it sounds oddly plausible."

They bought two air mattresses, a two-man pup tent, a set of nesting metal pans (for cooking budget meals along the road), two mugs, a dented green canteen, and a small used ice chest. When they returned to the car, Verity produced two clip-together knife-fork-spoon sets and a deck of cards—all pilfered when Max wasn't looking.

"Great," said Wilder. "I'm harboring a thief."

"He overcharged us for that rusty ice chest. I'm just evening out the trade."

Wilder consulted his notebook and road map. "There's a fair in Pennsylvania that's open for the rest of the week, but I'd rather not do all that crisscrossing across states."

"There's also the Mann Act to consider," Verity pointed out.

"The Mann Act?"

"The Feds frown on taking females across state lines for immoral purposes."

"Why wasn't Boyd arrested? That man should be jailed! Dot is barely 18."

"You should send a wire to J. Edgar Hoover."

"I would if I thought it would do any good. There's a fair down near Cincinnati that starts in two days. That might appeal to Boyd."

"I've always dreamed of visiting that town."

"Why's that?"

"I understand they make soap there. Perhaps I could get a bath. I smell like old mohair upholstery soaked in bug spray. With a bit of eau de mouse splashed on for piquancy."

Wilder handed her the map. "We need to head south on

Route 25. Tell me when to turn. And keep in mind this isn't a pleasure trip. We're on a serious mission."

"You are, buddy. I'm just taking a minor detour on the road to a better life."

They took Route 4 and connected to 25 in Dayton, home of the Wright brothers and the world's largest cash register factory. Soon they were back among rolling fields of waist-high corn.

"Boy, if you aren't fascinated by agriculture, it could get seriously dull living around here," she said.

"It's pretty though. Ohio is a very scenic state."

"I prefer the intersection of Broadway and 42nd Street. And why are all these barns exhorting us to chew Mail Pouch Tobacco? Why on earth would I want to do that?"

"I think that company paints your barn for free if you devote one whole side to their big ad."

"And these barn billboards persuade people to buy their product?"

"I guess it must. Lots of ballplayers chew 'cause they can't smoke on the field."

"A disgusting habit. Speaking of which, I had a thought about Dot the Bounder. She might not be living in sin."

"I'm sure she's not. She comes from a very respectable family."

"She might have married ol' Boyd. They may have tied the knot and are now honeymooning in his trailer."

"But she barely knows the guy!"

"The magic can happen fast. Some enchanted evening. Have you seen that new show 'South Pacific?' Their eyes might have met across a crowded room. Then they sang a duet among the Miracle Creme cans and all thoughts of Wilder S. Flint flew out of that dim girl's mind."

"Dolores is very intelligent. She won the all-city spelling bee in the seventh grade."

"You're probably going to receive a card soon telling you where to send the wedding gift."

"That's it, Verity! That's got to be it!"

"Oh, convinced you did I?"

"All along I've been assuming that Boyd was single. But what if he's married! What if it's the three of them in that trailer?"

"That sounds rather kinky. Not to mention tacky."

"No, it's Boyd and wife in the bedroom and Dot on the dinette! She's just working for them and helping out!"

"Then why hasn't she contacted you?"

"She may be trying to. She may have called or sent me a letter. I was only back in Erie for less than a day."

"I guess you'll have to phone your parents to find out."

"No, I can't face them. No way. You'll have to phone them instead."

"I get it. I say hi, I'm Verity. You don't know me, but I slept with your son last night and was wondering if you had any messages for him."

"No, you just say you're a friend of Dolores. Say you're calling to see if they'd heard from her."

"And if they have a letter addressed to you, then what?"

"Then I call back and have them read it to me. Then we all have a good laugh at this misunderstanding, and I drop you off at the nearest intersection."

"OK, Wilder. I'll make the call. It might be amusing to talk to the people who brought you into this world."

In a place called Blue Ball, Wilder pulled into a campground on a lake. Tent camping was $1 a night, showers were available, and there was a phone booth outside the cinder-block office. A sign at the entrance read: NO MOTOR-CYCLES. OUR GUARD IS ARMED. Wilder parked the Plymouth under some trees in a level grassy spot with a view of the lake.

"This is actually rather nice," said Verity. "I could live here. Well, for 24 hours at least."

Wilder wanted to crowd into the phone booth with her, but she told him to back off. The party on the other end of the line did most of the talking. Periodically Verity exclaimed, "Oh, really!" which Wilder found unsettling. After feeding in her fifth quarter, Verity said "bye-bye" and hung up.

"Your mother sounds very sweet, Wilder. She's quite worried about you. You should at least send her a postcard and let her know you're OK."

"I will if you will. I'm sure your parents are just as worried."

"I'll think about it. OK, here's the scoop. There's no word from your wayward girlfriend and no letter. Your mother talks to Dot's mother daily and she hasn't heard from her either."

"That is so strange!"

"That's not the half of it. Your father is in New Philadelphia."

"Why? Is he looking for me?"

"Apparently not. He's quite pissed at you. Your welding school doesn't give refunds. He got excused from picketing duty and has gone there to finish your course. He's learning to weld."

"What!"

"Yes, I understand his first project will be leg irons for you."

"Did you make that up?"

"Just the part about the leg irons."

"That is so like my father! He has to show me that he's the responsible one. As if I didn't have a very good reason for quitting that school."

"Do they do any welding on those screen doors?"

"Of course not. He's just doing that to show me up. He'll be lording it over me for the rest of my life. All about the $318 I would have wasted if he hadn't taken my place. Hey, I paid that tuition myself! I didn't ask him for a cent!"

Wilder was so upset he had to take his fishing pole down to the water and sit on the boat dock for two hours with no bait on his hook. Not that a worm would have changed the outcome. Like many bodies of water in Ohio, Blue Ball Lake was all fished out.

When Wilder returned, Verity had pitched the tent and was drying her hair with a plush towel from the Hotel St. Regis.

"The shower looks like something from a Soviet prison camp, the water only dribbles out, you have to feed in a dime every 30 seconds, and you could die waiting for the hot water."

"I've made up my mind, Verity. I've come to a decision."

"No fresh fish for dinner, huh?"

"I've decided to enlist in the United States Marines."

"Oh no you won't, Tiger. No one should make life-altering decisions in your state of mind. That's how World War I got started."

"It's my life. I guess I can enlist if I want to."

"Sorry. Not while I'm minding the store. We will do just what you planned. We will go to the fair, locate your girlfriend, and find out if she's as big a slut as she appears to be. Then you will consider your options and not do anything precipitous. You'd only be joining the Marines to get back at your parents and hide out from life. So forget it."

"Three of my high-school buddies are already down at Camp Lajeune."

"Then I guess Erie, Pennsylvania has filled its quota. Those guys can go learn to be brave fighting machines. You're intended for better things."

"Who says so?"

"Me for one. So shut up and start grilling those hotdogs. This girl is hungry."

Dinner was hotdogs and a pint of potato salad from the campground store. Like all store-bought versions it was overly sweet and the potatoes were under cooked. Not a problem for Wilder, who had too much on his mind to taste his food. He wanted to go swimming afterward, but hadn't packed a bathing suit. So instead of getting clean in the lake he had to face the dreary showers. When he returned, they went for a walk around the campground. Of the 100 or so camping spots less than a third were occupied. About half tents and half trailers. No fancy Spartans or Vagabonds. The lake was too small for water skiing, but a couple of the rental rowboats and canoes were in use. Kids were racing by on bikes and splashing in the water at the man-made sandy beach. Clangs and thumps could be heard from the horseshoes pits.

"With the passing of the horse I'm surprised that game hasn't faded away," said Verity, taking his arm. "It's seldom played in Manhattan."

"I got beaned by a horseshoe at Boy Scout camp. Only time I was ever knocked out."

"That's terrible. Was it deliberate?"

"No, wild pitch by a fat kid. I was about 40 feet off to the side tooling leather at a picnic table. Then bam, I was down for the count. I had a headache for a week."

Verity stifled a laugh. "So, let's hear about your high school."

"What's to tell? I'm glad it's over."

"Didn't you like any of your classes?"

"Typing class was OK I guess. At least I was learning a skill. And gym was tolerable except for all those calisthenics and running cross-country in a snowstorm in your shorts and T-shirt."

"If you hated school so much, why didn't you drop out?"

"I don't know. School was something you did. My friends were there. Dot was there. And I played sports. I made the varsity basketball team. I played shortstop on our baseball team. We won the regional title two years in a row. I batted fourth in the cleanup spot. I had to keep my grades up so I was eligible to play. How about you? I suppose you *liked* school."

"Sure, mostly. I went to an all-girls high school. The thing is you get 200 girls in one place and everything gets very competitive. Not just academically. You name it, we competed over it: straightest teeth, best dates, slimmest ankles, nicest elbows, most gracious mother. I scored poorly in that last category. It was all very intense. But every day you were fully engaged with life. You kind of get used to that intensity."

"All girls, huh? Did you ever go out with boys?"

"Of course. To dances and parties–the usual. We'd park by the shore and do a bit of close-quarters wrestling."

"You had sex with those guys?"

"We necked. They groped. Underwear got disarranged. I suppose you never got fresh with Dot."

"We had our moments. So you're not going to college?"

"I'm supposed to. I'm signed up to start at Berkeley in September. I got into five schools, but picked Berkeley because it was the farthest away from my mother."

"You must be pretty smart."

"Yeah, can't you tell?"

They stopped by the campground store and bought a newspaper and two postcards showing the Ohio state flag (only flag of the 48 states shaped like a pennant). Wilder checked the sports page for baseball updates: the Pirates weren't burning up the National League.

Later, when they were blowing up the air mattresses, a woman strolled by with a small fluffy dog on a leash.

"I hope you don't think I'm being nosy," she said, "but I was telling my Walter you folks look like newlyweds on your honeymoon. You just look so radiant."

"You guessed it," replied Verity. "Traditional June wedding, naturally. Just family and friends. Father said we had to economize so we limited ourselves to 600 invited guests. My dress was the dreamiest shade of robin's egg blue, and the groom's shoes and socks were dyed to match. All my bridesmaids carried flower baskets woven from their own hair. The ring bearers were my little twin sisters on roller-skates. They're only four years old and looked adorable. Didn't they, Felix darling?"

"Adorable. Yeah, right," grunted Wilder.

"Sounds lovely, dear. I don't mean to pry, but where's your wedding ring?"

"Oh, we took them off for safe keeping. I have a morbid fear of losing my diamond in the lake. It's over three carats and is quite blinding in normal daylight. Flawless, of course, like my complexion."

"Goodness, that sounds expensive."

"It's a family heirloom. Belonged to my dear Felix's grandmother. She was the niece of Cecil Rhodes of South Africa fame."

"And are you going home after leaving here?" she asked.

"Oh, no. We're on a mission to find the inventor of Miracle Creme. Do you know that product?"

"Oh, yes. We use it all the time. We feared my Walter was losing his hair. Now he rubs a pinch of Miracle Creme into his scalp every night before bed. His barber was amazed. I swear now he has nicer hair than Cary Grant."

"Oh, my. Cary Grant! You don't say! Felix, darling, did you hear that?"

"Yeah, I heard," sighed Wilder.

"You'll have to try that on your chest, dear. Confidentially, my husband has the chest of a nine-year-old girl. And I do like a manly chest. Of course, he likes his women buxom in the extreme so I guess we're even on that score.

"Marriage does require some compromises."

"That's what I keep telling him. But one doesn't wish to become a shrew."

"Well, I won't keep you dears. I hope you have a wonderful life together."

"We're certainly going to try! It's been heavenly so far!"

The woman and her dog continued on along the path.

"You sure can spin the tall tales," observed Wilder.

"I know. I'm bad. Just wind me up and off I go."

"You want the tent or the car?" he asked.

"I thought we were going to share the tent. It's advertised as a two man, but I don't think the stag rule is strictly enforced."

"Naw, we better not."

"Oh, OK. In that case I'll take the tent. It smells better."

"Right. That's fine with me. I'll oil up with the bug spray, then pass you the bottle."

"Good plan. Thanks. I was kidding about your chest."

"It could be brawnier."

"No, it's fine. Much nicer than mine, for example."

"No, yours is OK too."

Bedded down in the car, Wilder wrote this on his postcard:

Dear Mom and Dad,

I'm in Ohio and everything's fine. Sorry about borrowing Uncle Paul's car. It's running OK. I'm close to locating Dot. Will return after I talk to her.

Your loving son,

Wilder

On her postcard Verity wrote:

Dear family,

I'm in Ohio and seeing the sights. Now I know where corn comes from. Also cash registers. Please thank everyone for the graduation gifts. Will write again when I cross the Mississippi River. Berkeley here I come!

Not to worry,

V.

Chapter 3

Inspired by the roadside signs they were passing, Verity tried composing her own. "How's this, Wilder: HIS GAL LEFT TOWN. HE WEARS A FROWN. SHE HAD A DREAM. OF MIRACLE CREME. BURMA-SHAVE."

"It's supposed to relate to shaving," he pointed out.

She gave it some thought. "OK, here goes: HIS LIFE CAREENS. HE'S OFF TO THE MARINES. HIS GAL NOW SLEEPS. WITH UNSHAVEN CREEPS. BURMA-SHAVE."

"That hardly sells the product."

Her next effort: "WITH THE ARMY LOOMING. HE SKIPPED ALL GROOMING. NOW HIS GAL IS ROOMING. WITH A SALESMAN BOOMING. BURMA-SHAVE."

"That's OK."

"No, it still needs work. 'Salesman booming' sounds forced. How about this for lines three and four: WITH A CAD HIS GAL IS ROOMING. NOW HIS LOVE LIFE NEEDS EXHUMING?"

"Better, but you're just promoting shaving in general."

"Damn, I wouldn't want you as a client. Here's the best I can do: HE SHAVED IN THE LOO. WITH GREEN CANNED GOO. INSTEAD OF THE BEST. NOW ALL HIS HOPES ARE LAID TO REST. BURMA-SHAVE."

"That's pretty good."

"Pretty good? It's genius."

"How come they're all about me? Write one about you."

"Fair enough. Try this on for size: SHE SHAVED HER LEGS.

AND NOW HE BEGS. TO HIT THE SHEETS. FOR KINKY TREATS. BURMA-SHAVE."

"Not bad."

"God, you're a tough grader. Fortunately, I can do this all day. SHE SHAVED HER GAMS. AND NOW HE SLAMS. INTO HER TENT. WITH LUSTFUL INTENT. BURMA-SHAVE."

"That works for me. Where else do girls shave?"

"I expect your Dot is ruthlessly thorough. OK, how about this? SHE SHAVED HER PITS. TO GIVE HIM FITS. AND EVEN HER PUBES. TO INCITE THE RUBES. BURMA-SHAVE."

They both laughed. It was the first time she had heard him laugh.

"One more and that's it. SHE SHAVED DOWN THERE. SO SHOCKINGLY BARE. BUT WAS ONLY GAME. IF HE DID THE SAME. BUR-MA-SHAVE."

More laughter.

"That one, Verity, we should get printed on signs. Then set them up beside a road and see if anyone notices."

"I think they'd get noticed. Especially by the cops. Oops, I think we just missed our turn."

Back on the right road Verity reached over and smoothed his hair back over his ear. "So, Wilder, what do you want to be when you grow up? And don't say a Marine."

"I wish I knew, Verity. I don't think I want to be any-thing."

"I don't see many want ads for that job. And I doubt it pays well. Can't you narrow things down a little?"

"Well, I wouldn't want to work inside. Being cooped up in a building all day, that would be hell."

"Good. That narrows it some. You need an outside job. You're good at baseball. Why not play baseball profession-ally?"

"That's a joke. I'm generally considered the third best shortstop in my area. Even if I were the third best short-stop in the state, I doubt any pro scouts would look at me twice."

"How about baseball coach? Doesn't every high school and college employ one?"

"You got to have a college degree for that, Verity. I hate school."

"But majoring in physical education, is that really like school?"

"Sure it is. It's four years in the classroom. Boring lectures on the muscles of the body and God knows what else. I'd go nuts."

"So in your wildest fantasies, you can't think of a single job you'd like?"

"Maybe fur trapper. Heading off into the wilderness with your pack horses and Indian guide. But they're not buying many beaver pelts these days."

"That's your problem, Wilder. You were born in the wrong century."

"So what do you want to be, Verity?"

"I'm not sure. Maybe work for a newspaper. I'm sort of nosy and I like to snoop. I don't mind asking people embarrassing questions. I can kind of write. And I'm a wiz at typing. Except they'd probably stick me on the Society Page describing the frocks and headgear that prominent matrons wore to charity luncheons. I'd chafe at that, Wilder. I'd chafe severely. Sarcasm would creep into my stories and I'd get shown the door. You were born in the wrong century. And I was born the wrong sex."

"I wouldn't want to be a girl. Have guys mooning over you."

"I don't mind that part. It's not nearly as bad as it sounds."

Butler County Fair charged for parking and didn't care that Wilder was on leave from the 82nd Airborne. (Armed Forces Day was later in the week.) But it was Ladies Day so Verity got in for free. In the exhibition hall they watched a man demonstrate a miniature wood plane that employed a standard razor blade. It had hundreds of documented uses, but time constraints limited him to showing a mere dozen.

"That's a pretty nifty tool," said Wilder. "It can sure shave that wood. I'd buy one if I had the money."

"It's only a dollar, Wilder. I'll buy you one if you want."

"Naw, it'd probably just sit in a drawer. I don't do that much planing of wood. Let's keep going."

They were headed toward a flag-bedecked booth staffed by uniformed Marines, when Verity tugged on his arm.

"Wilder, look!"

Across the way was a stout woman carrying a flat green tin. Wilder accosted her at once.

"Excuse me, ma'am. Can I ask where you got that item?"

"Out by the cattle barn, son. There's a stand where they sell 'em."

They found the barn and spotted the stand, where a middle-aged man had attracted a small audience to hear his spiel. Verity pulled Wilder behind a pole.

"What are you planning to do, Wilder?"

"Go punch that bastard in the face."

"Let's pause here and think it over. At least wait until his show is done. There might be fewer witnesses to testify against you when you're charged with assault."

"I don't see Dot in that stand. He might have her bound and gagged in his trailer."

"But probably not. This is not very flattering for you, Wilder. She's left you for a guy who's at least 40, has a severe over-bite, and is wearing a toupee."

"How do you know that?"

"I know that because I'm not blind. And would you look at that!"

"What?"

"His ears are on backwards."

"Naw, they're just shaped funny."

"Still, I bet you'd have a very difficult time sneaking up on him from behind."

"I wasn't planning on doing that."

"Promise me you'll talk to him first, Wilder. You won't do anything rash."

"OK, I'll talk to the bastard."

Several people in the group lined up to purchase cans. After the money had changed hands, Wilder and Verity approached.

"OK, mister," he said. "I'm looking for Dolores Bateman. Where is she?"

"Who?"

"Dolores Bateman. Goes by the name Dot. You know who she is."

"Sorry, I don't know any Dots. You must have me confused with someone else. Now buy a can or move on."

"What did you do with her? Did you sell her into white slavery? Did you strangle her?"

"Get out of here, you nutcase, or I'll call a cop!"

"I'm making a citizen's arrest on you, mister. Right here and right now! You are in violation of the Mann Act."

"Kid, are you insane or what? I got a baseball bat here and I'll use it on your head!"

"Wait, Wilder," said Verity. "Look at the label on the can. It says Magic Creem not Miracle Creme. It's the wrong guy! He's selling a knock-off."

"I am not," he replied, offended. "I'll have you know that this is my very own secret formula. Unique in the entire world. My legions of satisfied customers assure me that it is far superior to any of the competition."

"Your name isn't Boyd?" asked Wilder.

"It certainly isn't. You must be looking for Boyd Wagstaph. And I am definitely not that charlatan!"

"So you know the guy?" asked Wilder.

"Unfortunately, I do."

"Is he at this fair?"

"Fortunately not."

"Do you know where he is?"

"Very far from me, I hope."

"Is he married?" asked Verity.

"Not very likely. I'm sure marriage would cramp his style."

"What does he look like?" asked Wilder.

"I don't know. He looks a bit like that limey actor, what's his name."

"Who?" said Wilder.

"You know, the one who got annoyed when that snooty rich dame broke his golf clubs."

"I don't know what the hell you're talking about."

"I do," said Verity. "You mean to say he looks like Cary Grant?"

"A bit, I suppose. Except he's built bigger and has better hair."

"How could he have better hair?" asked Verity. "Cary Grant has fabulous hair."

"Well, all the girls love his hair. Or so Boyd claims. I'm a bit envious myself, to tell you the truth. If I had hair like him, I bet I could move his weekly volume too."

"So you don't know anything about his fairs route?" asked Wilder.

"Sorry. I make it a point to avoid that guy. I do like selling to his repeat customers though. They sometimes get our products confused."

"Yeah, I wonder why," said Verity.

"How about a phone number where we can reach him?" said Wilder.

"Sorry, wrong guy to ask. Now if you excuse me, I'm trying to make a living here. I tell you what, here's a free can for your trouble. I suggest you apply a dab to that zit on your forehead."

"It's not a zit," replied Wilder, accepting the can. "It's a mosquito bite."

To divert Wilder from returning to the Marines' booth, Verity bought them both giant roasted turkey legs, which they gnawed on for lunch. They sat in adjoining wooden seats. You put a nickel in the slot and a concealed motor vibrated your tired feet.

"Did your girlfriend have a thing for Cary Grant?" she asked.

"Not that I noticed. But she never missed a Robert Taylor picture."

"He's married to Barbara Stanwyck."

"I guess Dot knew that. It didn't seem to put a damper on her enthusiasm for his movies."

"Was she a big-time reader of fan magazines?"

"Well, she worked part-time at Lakeside Drugs. They sold them there."

"His real first name is Spangler."

"Who, Cary Grant?"

"No, Robert Taylor. His real name is Spangler Taylor. Cary Grant's real name is Archibald Leach. Spangler ranks right up there with Wilder, don't you think?"

"I think I'm going to have a hard time competing with a guy who looks like Cary Grant."

"Except he sounds like a total cad. I doubt that infatuation will last very long if she has an ounce of sense–which, of course, she may not."

"I guess we should still try to find her. Just to make sure she's OK."

"You're a nice guy, Wilder. A really sweet guy."

"Yeah. And aren't we supposed to finish last?"

At Verity's insistence they spent a total of 50 cents to see the Monkey Speedway. Four monkeys in colorful track suits piloted little race cars around an electrified track. The bravest of the monkeys drove through a brick wall that was hinged to break apart upon impact.

"Isn't this the cutest thing you've ever seen?" Verity asked. "Here's the ideal outdoor career for you, Wilder. The monkeys bring in the customers and do all the work. All you have to do is collect the money. I bet it's a gold mine!"

"I don't know about monkeys, Verity. I hear they're pretty temperamental and like to bite people. You'd have to be heavily insured. And I think the smart ones can pick locks."

"Every job has its drawbacks, Wilder. You just have to keep an open mind."

"All the same, I think I'll skip the monkeys."

When they returned to the car, it wouldn't start. Wilder pushed the starter button, but nothing happened.

"What's the matter?" asked Verity.

"Battery died, I guess. It was on its last legs. Damn!"

"What can we do?"

"Get someone to jump us, I suppose. But it won't start the next time either. The sucker's dead. We need a new battery. That could cost 20 bucks or more. Son of a bitch!"

"Does this car take a special battery?"

"No, they're all pretty much the same."

"There are thousands of cars parked here, Wilder. And no one's around."

"Are you suggesting we swipe one?"

"Desperate times call for desperate measures."

"We'd need a wrench. Or at least a pair of pliers."

Verity rummaged in her duffel and extracted a large Crescent wrench. "Will this do?"

"Probably. Where'd you get that?"

"From the cab of that amorous trucker in Jersey. I knocked him upside the head with it, dislodging his hat."

"Jesus. Was the truck moving at the time? Did you kill him?"

"No and no. He had bought me a milkshake at a truck stop and decided it was payback time. But no girl wants to lose her virginity in a parking lot in Paramus, New Jersey. Especially to some sweaty stranger with beer breath. He was moaning when I left him. And definitely breathing. It was only a glancing blow. Much less forceful I expect than the clang of that errant horseshoe against your youthful skull."

"God, Verity. You might be a fugitive from the law!"

"That's why I kept the weapon in question. No sense leaving my fingerprints behind. I expect I won't be returning to New Jersey anytime soon."

"I think you should ditch that hat. It could be incriminating."

"But I like my hat. And you really need head protection in this Midwestern heat."

"We'll get you another one."

To keep it simple, they picked the new green Kaiser parked next to them as the donor. Wilder did the swap while Verity stood watch. He took the trouble to install his old battery in the Kaiser to divert suspicion. And he switched on its headlights to make it appear that the driver had forgotten to turn them off. With any luck no one might suspect that a crime had taken place.

The Plymouth started right up and displayed new electrical vigor. Wilder drove away at a sedate pace, resisting the urge to speed. Heading up Route 27 toward Oxford, Ohio he reached over and tossed Verity's Stetson out the open window.

"Better watch it, buddy," she snarled. "I still have my wrench."

"Not for long, Ma Barker. We're getting rid of that too."

In Oxford Wilder traded the nearly new wrench for half

a tank of gas. He bought Verity a soda from a grimy machine as consolation for her loss. A new banner pasted across its front asked "Why Take Less When Pepsi's Best?" The company's previous slogan, "Twice as Much for a Nickel," had been rendered untenable by postwar inflation.

Sipping her beverage in the shade of a rack of used tires, Verity was still thinking about the monkeys. "Here's a question for you, Wilder. Those monkeys: do they put on their little suits themselves or do the people have to dress them? Just how smart is a ringtail monkey?"

"I'm sure I have no idea."

"Do you think they enjoy their jobs? Do monkeys like to race around a track in swift little cars?"

"Probably so. Why not? I expect they like it as much as those drivers racing at the Indianapolis 500. Going fast is fun. They didn't look at all scared. I'm sure it's a lot more fun that sitting around in a cage all day."

"Well, don't think of taking up race-car driving. It's much too dangerous. You'd be better off in the Marines."

"I feel bad about that guy with the Kaiser. We're probably wrecking his day."

"That's the problem with crime, Wilder. It weighs on your conscience. He might have come to the fair with some girl he's trying to impress. Now they're stranded and he's looking bad. Although I doubt I would be swept away by a guy driving a Kaiser. It's such a funny-looking thing."

"Not my first choice in cars either."

"I hope that truck driver is recovering."

"I wouldn't waste any time worrying about him, Verity. He got what he deserved."

"True. But it's an ugly thing to have to deal with. Do men need it that badly they have to force themselves on not-so-alluring girls?"

"Some do, I guess. Accepting that milkshake from him was not so smart."

"So I learned. And now I've let you buy me a Pepsi. I suppose there'll be more hell to pay."

"You never know, Verity. Even the nice guys can turn on you."

They camped that night at the municipal campground in Camden, Ohio. It lacked a lake but offered a coin-op laundry. Wilder especially was getting behind in his laundry. If he ever did meet up with Dot, he didn't want to smell like he had just crossed the Isthmus of Panama by mule. The park also offered an ornate bandstand that would have been handy had they been traveling with an orchestra. A sign affixed to its side stated that it was not to be used for dining, dancing, or sleeping. Jumping from the stage also was prohibited.

Dinner was hotdogs again. All the ice had melted in the cooler, and Verity felt they should be consumed without delay.

"We need one of those little portable radios," she said, opening a can of asparagus that had been marked down on account of the dent. "I miss music."

"I hear they eat batteries. It takes a lot of juice to light up those little tubes."

"I'm the same way. Who's your favorite singer?"

"Uh, Dick Haymes I guess."

"He's married to Joanne Dru, but rumor has it that not all is well in the Haymes household."

"How do you know that?"

"I don't know. I just hear stuff. I might have read it in Winchell's column."

"What singer do you like?"

"Johnny Hartman. He's with Dizzy Gillespie."

"Never heard of him."

"He's new on the scene. I saw him at the Royal Roost. That's a club in New York. He has a rich baritone that just melts all your internal organs. Probably how you feel when Dot bats her eyelashes."

"Don't remind me."

They ate the limp green spears straight from the can with their fingers.

"I always thought I hated asparagus," said Wilder.

"It's time you outgrew those foolish notions. How are you on the dance floor?"

"Pretty much an embarrassment to all concerned."

"We may be able to fix that."

"I doubt it."

While their clothes tumbled promiscuously in the rotary dryer, they took a stroll around the campground.

"Campgrounds are great for people who like to snoop," said Verity. "You can peek into so many lives. Everything's out in public view."

"The folks in the trailers have more privacy. Except in the little teardrops 'cause they only crawl in those to sleep. I bet the Plymouth could tow a teardrop."

"I'd settle for one of those. Bedding down in your own tiny home on wheels. Just slightly larger than a casket. Like many urbanites I always sneered at vacationers in trailers. As a tent dweller I now see how mistaken I was. They can travel everywhere and still sleep in their own comfy bed. With screens on the windows to keep out the bugs. And a real kitchen. And even a toilet that's not a half a block away."

"Only your bigger trailers have that. And they can be a pain to tow," Wilder pointed out.

"Not a concern to me, dear. I'd let you do all the driving."

Loud hymn-singing was emanating from one of the older trailers. Its exterior had been redone like a church with applied gothic arches and traceries cut from thin hardboard. A hinged steeple cleverly folded upright on the roof when camped. The windows had been painted to suggest stained glass. A sign hanging by a chain on the front propane tank read: T.J. CARRUTHERS, MOBILE MINISTRY. JOIN US FOR PRAYER 24 HOURS A DAY. DO NOT KNOCK, JUST WALK IN! WE HAVE NOTHING TO HIDE. DO YOU?

"Reverend Carruthers must be a devout insomniac," said Verity. "Shall we return at two a.m. to test his sincerity?"

"You can, Varsity. Let me know in the morning how it turns out."

Since Verity was lacking a nickname, Wilder took it upon himself to provide one. She didn't seem to mind.

Even though they had just separated out their laundry and folded each other's underwear, the sleeping arrangements were the same as the night before.

Chapter 4

"Too bad they don't sell breakfast in cans," said Verity, attempting to scramble eggs over a fire fueled by yesterday's newspaper. "Where are we headed today?"

Wilder consulted his notebook and road map. "There's the Washington County Fair in Marietta. But it looks to be a long haul. Over 200 miles."

"Can your car make it that far with its lovely new battery?"

"We'll have to see."

Wilder decided on a route that bypassed the traffic-clogged big cities. "At least it's getting me closer to home if I do find Dot there," he said, outlining a route on the map that went via Wilmington, Chillicothe, and Athens. They would be traveling generally east across the southern part of the state.

"But it's opposite the direction I want to go," she pointed out.

"I could take you back up to U.S. 40 and drop you off, Varsity, if you'd rather."

"That's the meanest thing anyone has ever said to me."

"Just trying to be helpful."

They had their eggs with campfire toast and smoky tea. A few minutes later it started to rain, so their tent and other gear got stowed away wet. They took Route 725 to Gratis, where they stopped for ice and groceries.

"You'd think everything in this town would be free,"

said Verity as they packed away the supplies. "They need a refresher course in Latin."

"We've been passing a lot of fruit orchards. Too bad nothing's ripe yet. We might be able to get jobs as pickers."

"I'll look for an abandoned mattress on the side of the road. We could strap it to the roof to complete the Grapes of Wrath lifestyle."

"A day's hard work picking fruit never hurt anyone, Varsity. We could use the money."

"Just put me on the corner, Clyde. I can earn some fast cash at $2 a clip."

"I'm not so sure how fast it would be."

"That's the second meanest thing anyone's ever said to me. You're on a real roll today."

They went through Germantown, Franklin, Springboro, and Waynesville. Farmland and small towns with red-brick downtowns was the theme in this part of the state. Big white clapboard houses with broad porches. Green canvas window awnings shielded the dim interiors from glare and heat. All the yards were neatly mowed with a grape arbor, brick-edged pond, birdbath, or mirrored gazing globe as a point of interest. Roses and hydrangea were the flowers of choice, with the occasional honeysuckle climbing over a wire fence. Here and there they passed a pre-Civil War house of unadorned brick or stone built close to the road. Mounted to a few houses were tall, spindly masts topped by TV antennas trying to pull in a snowy picture from distant Columbus or Cincinnati.

The rain stopped and a weak sun peeked out periodically. Even on sunny days Ohio skies were awash in fluffy clouds. It had something to do with constant evaporation from the Great Lakes. Although it could be pointed out that California, in intimate embrace with the largest ocean in the world, was renowned for its clear blue skies (except in those car-clogged regions where smog had begun to obscure the sun and sting the eyes).

Verity looked over at the driver and frowned.

"I've figured out your problem, Wild One."

"What's that?"

"It's that girlfriend of yours. You grew up together. You saw her every day. You went to her birthday parties. You carried her books to school. You stared into her dreamy blue eyes and counted her freckles. You nuzzled her lily-white neck and breathed in her entrancing Woolworth's perfume. You slipped two straws into one soda at the malt shop and sucked away in a symbolic act of sexual congress."

"Now see here–"

"Don't interrupt. You thought you would be together forever. You can't conceive of life without her. You have no identity apart from her. None. Zilch."

"Yeah, I guess you're right, Varsity. So what do I do about it?"

"Well, you suffer."

"That's it? I suffer? And when does the suffering stop? When I get her back?"

"Maybe. If you're unlucky enough to do that."

"Why is it unlucky to be reunited with the girl I love?"

"That's for you to find out. Not for me to tell you."

"Dames. You never can get a straight answer out of 'em. And for your information Dot wears Jungle Gardenia perfume. I got it for her at Higbee's department store in downtown Cleveland. It was damn pricey."

"You *are* the proper gentleman caller aren't you? Well, don't be surprising me with any of those tacky streetwalker scents."

"You don't have to worry about that."

They took Route 28 to Chillicothe, where they stopped for lunch. Verity chose the restaurant, a place called Helen's

World Famous Siamese Pies. The big neon sign displayed beaming Siamese twins, joined at the side, each holding aloft a flashing pie.

"Why have I never heard of Siamese pies?" demanded Verity as Wilder pulled into the crowded parking lot. "Under what rock have I been living?"

Helen's menu was simple. It offered a selection of pot pies, baked in unique double-welled ceramic dishes. On one side was lunch (the pot pie), on the other side was dessert (a fruit pie). Verity ordered the chicken pot pie with cherry pie. Wilder went with the tuna pot pie with peach pie. Regulars were clued into the drill. When you raised your hand (signifying that you had consumed the lunch portion), a waitress walked over and dropped a big scoop of vanilla ice cream on your dessert side (if desired).

"I wish they had one of these in Erie," said Wilder. "I'd eat there every day."

"You mean until you were too fat to fit through the door. These crusts have enough lard in them to sink a battleship. I just found a layer of cheese under my chicken and carrots. Do you have any idea how many calories we're consuming? Look around you. We're the only people in the place under 200 pounds."

Helen herself came over to inquire how they were enjoying lunch.

"It's terrific," said Verity. "My friend here was wondering if your chef was available for marriage."

Helen laughed. "I'll see if she's interested. I hope you don't mind that she's an elderly colored lady."

"No problem," said Verity. "He's very flexible when it comes to pie."

When they crossed the bridge over the Hocking River and entered Athens, Verity suggested that they stop and look around.

"I always wanted to visit Athens, and this may be my only chance. I hope some of the natives speak English. Which way do you suppose is the Parthenon?"

They walked around the verdant campus of Ohio University, where chubby band leader Sammy Kaye had learned to swing (musically). Wilder was impressed to learn that the owner of the Pittsburgh Pirates was another distinguished alumnus. They strolled on to downtown where the marquee of the Athena Cinema was advertising "The Big Steal" starring Robert Mitchum and Jane Greer.

"Look, Wildest," said Verity. "They made a movie about our criminal careers. Let's go see it. We'll count it as our first official date."

"Oh? Are we dating now?"

"We'll go dutch. You buy the tickets and I'll buy the popcorn."

The movie was a dark tale about Mitchum meeting up with Jane in Mexico while tracking down stolen Army payroll. Sinister types were out to kill them, but after some double-crosses and hot gunplay, Bob and Jane won the day (and presumably each other).

"I could marry Robert Mitchum," said Verity as they exited the theater. "No courtship required. All he has to do is send me a telegram, and I'll be on the next bus to Hollywood. We could get married the same day I arrive. Just a simple ceremony. William Holden can give me away. Farley Granger can be best man. Lauren Bacall can be my matron of honor. We'll spend our wedding night in the bridal suite of the Ambassador Hotel. What do you think, Wild Bug?"

"Sounds OK to me. I'll even chip in for your bus ticket."

"That's very generous of you."

"Isn't he already taken?"

"We could work something out. His wife is named Dorothy, but goes by the nickname Dolores."

"Is that true?"

"No. That was a joke. I forgot you were from the land of deep snow and shallow thinking."

They found a campground down-river in the little town of Coolville, Ohio. Verity expected it to be jammed with hep cats and jive dudes, but found it sparsely occupied by the usual tent-and-trailer crowd. No one was smoking reefer or pounding out bop tunes on bongo drums.

They found a spot by the Hocking River and erected their soggy tent, which had acquired a noticeable mildew odor.

"I hope this thing airs out," said Verity. "It smells like your girlfriend's twat."

"What did you say? demanded Wilder.

"I said it smells like your girlfriend's feet. What of it?"

"Oh. I thought you said something else."

"You must have a dirty mind. And why haven't you shown me a photo of her?"

"You never asked."

Wilder removed his wallet and extracted what looked like a photo taken for a high-school yearbook.

"Nice," said Verity. "I like that bare shoulders look. I bet it was a big distraction in math class. Is she modeling her look on Rita Hayworth or Victor Mature?"

"All the girls wear that top for the photo, Varsity. It's supplied by the photographer."

"Yeah, she's pretty. And nicely stacked from the looks of it, although they cropped right across things. You should mail this photo to M.G.M. They might invite her out for a screen test."

"She wants to be a nurse."

"Right. She would."

Verity said she was too queasy to think about dinner. She left for the shower building, while Wilder made himself a fast cheese sandwich. She returned looking glum.

"I've got some good news, Wildest. I'm not pregnant. The bad news is I might be a trifle homicidal for a few days."

"Was there a possibility you might be pregnant?"

"Only if you had sneaked into my tent and had your way with me while I slept. I'm quite a sound sleeper. You might keep that in mind."

Wilder studied his map. "Coolville is right next to the towns of Torch and Frost. It's like they can't decide whether to be hot, cold, or cool."

"Ohio is a such a whimsical state. I expect it's to relieve the tedium of daily life."

"This river meets the Ohio River a mile or two east of here. Marietta is right on the Ohio River. I think it floods there sometimes. We'll probably see some river traffic tomorrow. You know: barges and such. It's a major commercial waterway."

"Good to know. Now I have a reason to live. I was beginning to have my doubts."

"I wonder if this river has any fish in it."

"It seems to have plenty of soapsuds in it. Why's that?"

"I think it's from the detergents people wash their clothes in now. It washes into the rivers and froths up."

"Such a pretty state and all the rivers are polluted."

"Ohio has lots of industry. That's to be expected."

"Is it? If lightning struck and you actually caught a fish, would it be safe to eat?"

"Probably not. You have to be careful where you fish these days."

"I'll stick with hotdogs. Exotic animal by-products beat factory-runoff fish in my book. Can you blow up my air mattress tonight, Wildness? I'd try, but I think it would kill me."

"Sure, OK. Want to play some cards?"

"No, I just want to moan and feel sorry for myself."

"Dot's never bothered much by her monthlies."

"That's what I like about you, pal. You always know the right thing to say."

Sluggishness in one party delayed their departure the next morning. Eventually, they got on the road to Marietta. Verity felt a need to talk.

"Wildest, we've know each other for quite some time now."

"Not very long actually."

"You've had time to observe me. What are my qualities that you feel would make me attractive to a man? Be honest."

No response from the driver.

She went on, "You don't have to enumerate them in order of importance. Just toss them out as they occur to you."

"Well, you have, uh, a nice smile."

"All right, that's a start. We'll put that down toward the bottom of the list. What else?'

"Uh, you're smart."

"I'm not sure men value that in a date. In fact the preponderance of evidence suggests that men avoid intelligent girls like the plague. Go on."

"You've got a shapely little can. No offence."

"You finally noticed that, did you? I was beginning to wonder. Anything else?"

"You're not fat."

"And not likely to get fat after the honeymoon. All my brothers are rail thin. My mother is not enormous. Please continue."

"Your eyebrows are not overly plucked. Guys really don't go for the bald forehead look."

"Such minutia is not helpful. I can see you're having trouble here. OK, here are some of my attributes that you missed: I have quite elegant hands. My nose really cannot be faulted on any point. I am above average in height as are you. Were I to fill out a bit I could be quite statuesque. I am a good listener and take a real interest in people. My hair, although brown and not artificially hued like Lana Turner's, is remarkably full and soft in texture. My facial bone structure has been compared favorable to that of Katherine Hepburn and Gene Tierney."

"By who?"

"Well, by my mother, but she is by nature quite a critical person. She doesn't pass out the compliments wholesale. Were you to see me in nylons and high heels, you would be impressed that I have quite glamorous legs. I am loyal to a fault. I have 20-20 vision. My teeth are straight and gleaming white. I brush with a name-brand tooth powder. I have a good sense of humor. I am not normally a depressed person. Except in high mosquito season I smell quite girlish. I am adventurous enough to undertake a cross-country trip on my own. I can spell–probably better than your spelling-bee champion. I am artistic and have lovely handwriting. I can make awkward people feel at ease. I'm lively and interesting at parties and would make a good hostess. Although I find most children to be a severe trial, I have the makings of a good mother. My health is generally robust. I manage my finances well and am not a spendthrift. In short, I am quite a dish. Do you see my point?"

"You're an attractive girl. Yeah, I get it."

"Good. I just felt we should clear up that issue. Any questions?"

"Is that a river to the right over there?"

"Yes. I believe it is the mighty Ohio."

"Good. We're on the right road."

Marietta was a pleasant river town with an imposing courthouse and a long steel bridge that crossed over to West Virginia. Wilder parked downtown and loaded up on motor oil and brake fluid in an auto parts store.

"What's with all the brake fluid?" asked Verity. "Are your brakes bad? Is that why you drive so slow?"

"They're not that bad. They just leak a bit. If we come to any steep hills, I suggest you keep your hand on the door lever in case you have to jump for it."

"Oh my. More good news. Let's go in this shop. I need to make an emergency purchase."

For not being a spendthrift Verity amazed Wilder by blowing nearly $4 on assorted chocolates. Nor did she seem inclined to share.

"Don't look at me like that, Wild Bill. If you guys were visited by this curse, you'd be succumbing to your cravings too."

The Washington County Fair proved just as disappointing as the others. No Miracle Creme vendors were seen.

"I don't get it," said Wilder, biting into a deep-fried sausage roll from a stand near the midway. It was served in a nest of sauerkraut in a paper cone. "Where is that guy?"

"It does seem like we should have run into him by now," said Verity. "How many counties does this state have?"

"Eighty-eight, I think."

"Damn! Do they all have fairs?"

"I expect they do. Plus, ol' Boyd could be in Pennsylvania for all we know. Aren't you having lunch?"

"You haven't been seeing me at my best lately, Wildness. I don't need to detract from my allure with convulsive vomiting."

"Shall we hit the road?"

"Not until we've seen the Guillotined Girl sideshow."

"You really want to see some girl get her head chopped off?"

"Why not? I missed out on the French Revolution. And it only costs a quarter."

The guillotining took place on an elevated platform in a dark tent. A rope strung on poles kept the spectators a respectable distance back. The intended victim was an attractive young miss in a low-cut top. A fellow dressed in black and wearing a hood gave a short history of the guillotine. It was deemed in the 18th century a humane innovation for offing folks. Much quicker than burning them at a stake. Next he read a proclamation condemning the girl to death for her crimes. He didn't go into specifics, but she must have been a bad apple and wasn't showing much remorse. He seized the prisoner and dragged her over to the machine. She didn't protest or struggle that much considering her fate, but then she went to her death dozens of times a day.

She settled into the block, giving everyone an eyeful as she bent over. She let out a whimper, the executioner pulled a rope, and down hurtled the polished steel blade. A bright light flashed, there was a chop and a thump as something heavy fell into a large basket. Nearly all the spectators gasped. One woman screamed. Verity bit into a chocolate from her sack. No one fainted. The man picked up the severed head by its hair and put it on a table. There didn't seem to be much blood. The disembodied girl opened her eyes and looked around. She said, "Ouch, that hurt!" and everyone laughed. She said she hoped they liked the show and to come back soon. Then the ticket seller opened a tent flap and everyone exited into the bright sunshine.

"How do you suppose they did that?" marveled Wilder.

"It was pretty clever. I think the bright light blinded us momentarily so we couldn't see clearly. You notice how quickly they did things. Still, I got my money's worth."

"Yeah, me too," yawned Wilder.

"How did you sleep last night?" she asked.

"Not well as usual."

"Could be unrelieved sexual tension. Want to go back to the car and take a nap?"

"We'd fry in this heat."

"Then let's go find some shade. I'm beat."

They found a cellar under an exhibition hall with an unlocked door. It was a storeroom for Civil Defense supplies. They stretched out on some bundles of (empty) sandbags. The room was dim and cool; they soon fell asleep.

When Verity woke up, Wilder was gone. She bolted upright and looked around. A moment later the door opened; Wilder was back.

"Oh, you're awake," he said.

"I'm awake. Where did you go?"

"I was finding a rest room."

"How is it out there?"

"Still hot but there's a breeze now."

"Good. Let's blow this joint."

When they returned to the car, Verity had an announcement to make.

"OK, Wildness. It's been fun, but this is where I say good-bye."

Wilder looked stricken. "You mean you're leaving?"

"Yeah, I've got a long way to go and I'm not making much progress in that direction. Can you haul my duffel out of the car?"

"If I said something to offend you, Varsity, I didn't mean to."

"Naw, everything's fine. I hope you locate that girl of yours before she's married and has a couple of kids."

"Thanks. We'll have to see."

"So I guess this is it. We'll never see each other again."

"I don't know. If the Army or Marines send me to California, is it OK if I look you up?"

"I guess so. Why would you want to do that?"

"Well, aren't you my friend? Don't you like me?"

"Do you like me?"

"Sure I do. You've been good company. I'll miss you."

He held out his hand. She didn't grasp it.

"OK, Wild Man. You passed the test."

"What?"

"This was only a test. I'm not leaving. You passed. I'm giving you a grade of D+, but you passed. You said just enough to keep me from saying sayonara to you and your flaming Death Car. Had you moved to extract my bag, or offered me a lift to the highway, you would have flunked big time. Such enthusiasm for my leaving could not have been borne. Confidentially, you'd have scored higher with some tears or at least an offer of a hug. A heartfelt kiss, of course, would have dramatically upped your score."

"What would it take to ace your test?"

"Hysterical wailing and pleading. Maybe some rending of garments. Keep that in mind for the next time."

"Your garments or mine?"

"Doesn't matter to me. Take your pick."

Chapter 5

They found a campground across the river in Williamstown, West Virginia that was only 50 cents a night. Not a place the Rockefellers would stay, but the section for tent campers offered a view of the river and railroad tracks. Every so often a long freight train chugged by, huffing black smoke. Verity found a well-worn copy of *Forever Amber* in the recreation hall and was soon engrossed in her book.

"That sure is a thick book," commented Wilder, opening a can of corned-beef hash. "How many pages does it have?"

Verity flipped to the last page. "Only 972. Apparently the original manuscript of the novel was five times longer, but the publisher felt some trees should be left on the planet."

"What's it about?"

"It's about a girl named Amber St. Clare in 17th century England who sleeps her way to a better life. So far that strategy hasn't been working for me."

"Sounds kind of risque."

"I certainly hope so. Shall I bookmark the pages with sex scenes for you?"

"Sure, why not? I doubt I'd ever get through a book that thick."

"It's unfortunate Readers Digest doesn't offer such a service: best-sellers condensed of everything except the naughty bits."

"I'd sign up for that. It could be a real time-saver."

A poster in the recreation hall advertised an ice cream social that evening in the town's Tomlinson Park. Sponsored by the fire department with homemade cakes and donated ice cream.

Considerable hectoring by Wilder was required to get Verity to put down her book and undertake the short stroll to the park. Chinese lanterns had been strung from tree to tree and long tables laid out. Firemen and their wives were serving up paper plates of cake and ice cream. Numerous strollers and babes in arms gave evidence of the baby boom underway. A clown on a unicycle was entertaining the bigger kids. A uniformed brass band was performing rousing tunes.

"God, what a wholesome scene," said Verity. "It's like a cover of the *Saturday Evening Post* come to life. It's enough to make a girl gag."

"I don't suppose you'd be interested in a piece of German chocolate cake," said Wilder.

"I might be. If you twisted my arm. And paid, of course."

Wilder bought two slices and they found a place to sit at one of the tables. They shared the table with a friendly couple who introduced themselves.

"Are you from Marietta?" asked the gal.

"No, we're from Fairbanks, Alaska," said Verity. "We're on our way to Brooklyn, where my husband's got a tryout with the Dodgers. He's a shortstop with a sizzling curve ball. In Alaska they call him the white Jackie Robinson."

"Uh, not quite," said Wilder, keeping his head down and concentrating on his cake.

"Jackie Robinson plays second base," noted the man.

"And what do you do?" asked Verity.

"I'm a molder at Fenton."

"What do you mold?"

"Glass. It's a glass factory."

"Would you say that is more interesting work than welding?"

"Definitely. There are lots of challenges in molding glass. You have to keep on your toes."

"You hear that, darling? That's something to consider. Wilder's been thinking of taking up welding if baseball doesn't pan out."

"I expect there are more job opportunities in welding," said his wife. "You have to know someone to get hired on at Fenton."

"Isn't that how it always works?" said Verity. "It's a wonder anyone gets on in this world."

Walking back to the campground, Wilder told her about his father's accident.

"The factory was busy with war contracts. Lots of compulsory overtime. First they made ammo boxes, then they made parts for gliders."

"What were the gliders for?"

"The Allies used them as troop and cargo carriers for the Normandy invasion. They were towed by C-47s. The framework was steel tubing, but they had lots of wooden parts. My dad's factory had to make thousands of identical parts. It was very repetitive and mind-numbing work. They'd rough out the blanks on band saws, then use shapers to conform them to patterns. That's a big machine with a flat table and sharp, whirling blades mounted to a vertical spindle."

"Sounds nasty."

"Yeah, it's probably the most dangerous machine in the shop. You have to stay alert when you're using it. Anyway, my dad was tired, the blades had lost their edge, and the piece he was shaping had a concealed knot. The blades dug into the knot and he lost control."

"What happened?"

"It took off his little finger on his right hand. It nicked the next finger too, but he pulled away in time. He was back at work four days later."

"That's remarkable. Does he still work at that machine?"

"No, he's a supervisor now. He mostly writes reports and tries to meet his production quotas. I'm not sure how much the guys on his shift like him. He's kind of a hard-ass."

"His accident didn't mellow him?"

"Just the opposite, I'd say. So he's trained himself to use his left hand. He keeps his right hand mostly in his pocket these days."

"He must be sensitive about his disfigurement."

"It's only a pinkie finger. I say what's the big deal?"

"Have you discussed that with him?"

"Nah. You don't talk about things like that with my dad."

"What do you talk to him about?"

"The usual stuff: sports, the weather, the cost of living, my ever-cloudy future."

"Perhaps that's why you lack career ambitions, Wildness. You associate work with injury, pain, blood, and amputation."

"I don't know, Varsity. I just think most jobs are boring."

"That's why operating a Monkey Speedway would be perfect for you. Those monkeys would keep you on your toes."

"Drive me crazy is more like it."

By next morning Verity was on page 112 of her book and too engrossed to make breakfast. Wilder soft-boiled the eggs and made tea from the same water.

"I'm going off to see if I can get some money," he announced, when he returned from washing the dishes.

"You're not planning to stick up a liquor store are you?" she asked, looking up from her book. "I really don't wish to be the target of a multi-state manhunt and die in a hail of gunfire like Bonnie and Clyde."

"No stickups today, Varsity. I'm leaving the felonies to you. If I'm not back by lunch time, will you be OK?"

"I'll cope. There's a fellow in a teardrop trailer across the way I'm hoping to seduce."

"Good luck on that. Well, I guess I'll be off."

"It's our first separation, Wildness. Aren't you going to kiss me good-bye?"

"Uh, OK."

He gave her a warm kiss full upon the tip of her nose.

He took the car and was gone all day. Verity was beginning to fear that she'd been abandoned. Wilder returned in the early evening with Chinese take-out. He'd been washing windows all day. He told her about it as they dined.

"If you just knock on someone's door and ask if they need any work done, you never get anywhere. You have to offer a specific service. And housewives don't like to wash windows. So I went to a hardware store and bought a squeegee and a bucket. The squeegee was $1.98 and the bucket was 49 cents. Then I found a prosperous-looking neighborhood in Marietta and started knocking on doors."

"Very resourceful, Wild One. How much did you charge?"

"My base price was 20 cents a window. That's only for washing the outside. If the yard was mowed and the bushes neatly trimmed or they had a Packard parked in the drive, I might quote a higher price like 30 or 35 cents."

"How savvy of you. That's called charging what the market will bear."

"Right. If I were back in Erie, I'd have brought my own ladder. But I'm on the road, so I had to use anything I could scrounge out of their garages or basements. Mostly spider-infested widow-makers."

"What's that?"

"Your widow-maker is a rickety old stepladder. I climbed

some real antiques today. Anyway, I made over 18 bucks and I have another job set for tomorrow. A lady wants her garage straightened. It's racking to one side and her doors are binding. She's having trouble getting her Studebaker out. She's paying me $30 to straighten it."

"How does one straighten a crooked garage?"

"I'm not exactly sure, but I'll figure it out. I think I may be able to winch against a tree. She'll have to pay for the rope though."

"You're so enterprising, Wildest. I admire that. In a place where you are a total stranger you manage to make money. I doubt I could have done anything except panhandle on a street corner. Is that how you saved all that money for welding school? By being entrepreneurial?"

"No, I worked for it. I had a paper route. Had to get up at the crack of dawn seven days a week. After school I'd deliver groceries on my bike. I also worked at the store on Saturdays stocking and bagging."

"That sounds exhausting. And so Dickensian. I'm surprised you weren't sorting coal in a mine at age seven."

"It wasn't bad. I got used to it. Snowy mornings in January were about the worst. You know, delivering papers in the freezing dark. I did get afternoons off when we had baseball games scheduled. What jobs have you had?"

"Living with my brothers and mother was my job. I should have been richly compensated by the state for that ordeal."

"What did you do for spending money?"

"I got it the old-fashioned way. From my generous father. He was inclined to indulge his only daughter."

"How's Amber St. Clare doing?"

"She's currently coping with an outbreak of bubonic plague. It hasn't put much of a damper on her love life."

The next afternoon Wilder suddenly returned, looking

distraught. They packed hastily and sped away from the park. Three minutes later they had crossed the bridge into Ohio and were motoring north on Route 77 at close to the legal limit.

"Any cops following us?" asked Wilder, anxiously checking his rear-view mirror.

"I don't see any. What happened! Did you stick up a bank? Did you kill someone?"

"It was that damn garage. Bugs had gotten to the frame. Powder post beetles from the looks of it. I told the lady, but she said it was fine. And she didn't want me leveraging off any of her precious trees. So I was giving it a tug with the Plymouth."

"Uh-oh. That doesn't sound good."

"Hey, I was being careful. I was going slow. Just nudging it along. I got it nearly straight. Then, boom, it collapsed like a house of cards. Big cloud of dust. Flat as a pancake. Surprised the hell out of me."

"You wrecked her garage! What did she do?"

"She wasn't there. She was off taking her daughter to piano lessons. I just hope that piano teacher is over in the next county."

"Does she know what your car looks like?"

"Sure she does. But I doubt she took down my license number."

"But how many old brown Plymouths with Pennsylvania plates can there be around here?"

"Not many, I'm sure. That's why we have to make tracks. We have to vamoose out of southern Ohio–for good. A whole morning's work and I never got my 30 bucks."

"You should have stuck to window washing. We could stop somewhere and swipe some Ohio plates."

"I don't think so. Jesus, Varsity, with you it's one felony after another."

"Hey, you're the garage wrecker not me. So where are we going?"

"There's a fair up in Zanesville. It starts the day after tomorrow."

"Oh damn!"

"Jesus, Varsity. What's wrong?"

"I left my book behind!"

"Is that all? I thought you saw a cop."

"They're threatening to throw Amber into debtors' prison. Her life is in crisis. She's knocked up, and the man she loves is off at sea."

"Ah, we'll get you another book, Varsity."

"You bet you will. And another hat too. I've had it with your empty promises."

Driving straight through on 77, they reached Zanesville by late afternoon. Two cops on loud Indian Scout motorcycles passed them along the way, but they were hunting bigger game than garage vandals on the run. Still, they gave a fright to the Plymouth occupants, who were beginning to regret their life of crime. Back on U.S. 40, Wilder drove over a Y-shaped bridge and parked out of sight down an alley.

A thrift shop run by volunteers in the basement of a Methodist church had a broad-brimmed hat that Verity found acceptable. Priced at 25 cents, which Wilder paid. He also purchased orange-striped bathing trunks for 15 cents, which Verity speculated had been owned previously by a "color-blind sponge diver." She bought several blouses and shorts she deemed suitable for "utilitarian camp wear in the muggy Midwest." She asked the white-haired gal at the cash register where she could find a copy of *Forever Amber*.

"I really couldn't say, miss. We wouldn't carry such a book even if it were donated. I doubt the library has a copy. You could try Sturtevant's on Main Street. They have a book department."

It turned out the library did have a copy. Verity slipped it into her bag and walked out with it.

"The crime spree goes on," muttered Wilder.

"I'm doing them a favor," she retorted. "This town is straight out of an Andy Hardy movie. They don't need to be corrupted by Kathleen Winsor's trashy prose."

"Then why are you reading it?"

"I'm a sophisticated New Yorker. I'm already corrupted. Besides, libraries expect to lose a certain number of books to pilferage. It's to encourage an interest in literature. Do you like my new hat? Who do you think I look like: Hedy Lamarr or Loretta Young?"

"Do I get any more choices?"

"Sorry, no."

"I guess Loretta Young."

"Thanks. I would have picked her too. Although I do have Hedy Lamarr's chin. The resemblance is uncanny. I'm surprised you haven't commented on that."

"Whose chin do I have?"

"Jimmy Stewart's. I noticed it two seconds after we met. But I expect your Dot already has pointed that out."

"Not that I recall."

"Now that surprises me. More proof of her indifference. I'm amazed you stuck with her as long as you did. Say, about that garage you demolished."

"What about it?"

"It occurred to me that weakened as it was it might have blown down in a strong wind and wrecked that lady's nice Studebaker."

"I guess so. It might have."

"Almost any crime you can think of can be excused on the basis that you're doing someone a favor."

"Even murder?"

"Of course. There are always a few folks who are happy

to see the victim go. I bet that truck driver's wife would not have been entirely displeased if I had put more muscle behind that wallop–especially if he was well-insured."

"I don't know, she might of loved him."

"Not likely. Believe me his creepiness factor was off the charts. And that guy whose battery you swiped: the girl he was trying to impress might have been completely wrong for him. Our timely intervention may have saved him from a disastrous marriage."

"It's possible, I suppose. Oh, I figured out what happened with that garage."

"What?"

"That rope I was using had too much stretch in it. You could only put a certain amount of tension on it, and then it started acting like a giant rubber band. Next time I'll use a chain or steel cable."

"It's outdoor work, Wildest. You could make a career out of it. You could become known coast-to-coast as the King of Garage Straighteners. You could advertise on the radio late at night when rates are cheapest. You could reach all those insomniacs worrying about their leaning garages."

"Hell, I'd prefer it to washing windows. Probably pays better too."

Chapter 6

They found a campground on the Licking River north of town. It was one of two rivers that met under the Y bridge. Wilder straightened up the mess made by their sudden departure, erected the tent, blew up the air mattresses, started the fire, and got dinner going. Verity read her book.

"I'm getting tired of doing all the work around here," he grumbled. "When is this thing of yours going to be over?"

Verity looked up from her book. "This thing, as you put it, is nature's way of reminding females that we got the short end of the stick. Reinforced, of course, by all the other ways we are daily oppressed. You should be happy I have this book to keep me occupied. Normally I'm given to strangling children and stomping small animals. I should be back to my usual congenial self tomorrow or the next day."

"Is there anything I can do?"

"Just go on being your normal sweet self."

After dinner they got invited to join a group of men, women, and kids playing softball on a field behind a derelict barn.

"Want to come?" asked Wilder.

"You go, honey," she replied. "I'm tired and I can feel the baby kicking."

"Uh, right."

The game went on until it was too dark to see. Beer and pretzels were consumed; everyone got at least one hit, and nobody was keeping score.

By next morning Verity was feeling better and had fewer than 100 pages to go.

"How are things with Amber?" asked Wilder, cooking breakfast.

"Looking up. She's out of Newgate Prison and making it big as an actress. She's the Vivian Leigh of Restoration England. But it's not looking good for her getting back together with Bruce."

"Bruce?"

"He's the swashbuckling father of her kid. Did I embarrass you last night?"

"When?"

"With my allusion to baby-kicking."

"Naw, I played right along. I told them you were thrilled to be expecting. The girls gave me some grief for hogging the car while you slept on the ground."

"As well they should. What's the plan for today?"

"Window washing for me. You'll be on your own again."

"Try not to knock down any more buildings. And stay off those widows."

"You mean widow-makers?"

"No. Those lonely young war widows."

Wilder returned with $19 profit and a bag of miniature burgers. They transported better than the French fries, which were soggy and limp. Verity had finished her book and regained her appetite.

"I don't see why that book was condemned," she said, helping herself to another burger. "There were only 70 references to sexual intercourse, 39 illegitimate pregnancies, and seven abortions."

"Sounds quite tame to me," he replied.

"Speaking of which, I've been thinking about your problem."

"Which one?"

"Your absconding girlfriend problem."

"Oh, that one. What about it?"

"There's only one sure-fire way to fix a broken heart."

"What's that?"

"Have sex with someone else. It sort of singes away those lingering attachments. It readies the heart for its new occupant. Kind of like repainting an apartment for the next tenant."

"And I suppose you're volunteering for the job."

"The thought had crossed my mind. But let's face it: neither of us has much experience in that area. When you're having your first time, it's helpful if someone knows what they're doing. If we tried it, our fumbling enthusiasm could go awry. The trauma could be everlasting. You might wind up one of those lifelong bachelors who collects stamps. I might become an embittered spinster living alone with my canary and potted plants."

"I'm not sure even lousy sex is that bad. So what do you suggest?"

"I suggest you visit a brothel."

"What!"

"You hire a pro. It's just like learning to weld. You go to someone who knows how to handle a torch. Otherwise, you're likely to get burned."

"And what makes you think they have a brothel in this podunk town?"

"Every town of any size has at least one. How do you think men cope whose wives would rather do needlepoint?"

"I thought they all hung out at the VFW hall and drank."

"That's only the older ones."

"And how do I locate this mythical cathouse?"

"Easy. You call a cab."

"Why should I do that? I've got a car."

"You call a cab and say to the driver, 'I'm new here. Where does a guy go to get laid in this burg'?"

"And the cab driver is supposed to know?"

"Of course. They all get kickbacks from the madams for the johns they bring in. It's standard practice in the industry. How do you think taxi drivers pay the rent?"

"What about diseases? You wouldn't believe the scary movies coach showed us in boys' gym."

"No problem. You wear a condom."

"Which I get where?"

"Not to worry. I've got a dozen in my duffel. I raided my oldest brother's stash before I left."

"You were planning to be busy on this trip?"

"A girl has to be prepared for contingencies. So, you agree to my plan?"

"I'm trying to figure out what's in it for you."

"I'm just trying to ease your emotional suffering, Wild One. Breakups are tough. It's no fun hanging out with a miserable guy who can't sleep. You could nod off at the wheel and kill us both."

"Yeah, I could be better company. And maybe more alert. But if I weren't miserable, I wouldn't be on this trip. And you'd be a missing person buried in some Indiana corn field."

"Not likely. I always land on my feet. Really, Wild Thing, I'm only thinking of your welfare."

"So you say. But knowing you there's got to be an angle. Are you by any chance thinking I'll go into town, have sex, get some experience, decide I like it, and start pestering you?"

"That thought never crossed my mind. Honest."

"Anyway, I'm not sure I have enough money for this night out. What are pros charging these days?"

"Around here I'd be surprised if the tab came to over $5. I'm even willing to chip in. I'll send you off with two condoms and $5 from my personal reserves."

"There's the cab ride there and back too."

"OK, I'll chip in $10. Do you want me to come along and hold your hand?"

"You really think this will help me feel better?"

"It's worked for thousands of years for millions of men. Why shouldn't it work for you?"

"OK, I'll think about it."

"Well, don't think about too long 'cause I already phoned for a cab. He's picking you up at eight o'clock sharp."

Wilder returned well past dark. He said he was tired and didn't want to talk. Ignoring Verity's protests, he brushed his teeth and retired to bed in the car–locking the doors and rolling up the windows. She sighed and crawled into her tent.

The next morning at breakfast she pried the story out of him.

"In the first place that cab driver was shocked and offended by my question. This is Ohio after all, not some sordid big city."

"So what happened?"

"He drove me to this kind of seedy-looking bar. He said somebody in there might be able to assist me. I went in and, not being of legal drinking age, requested a root beer. The bartender looked me over and asked what the hell I was doing in there. I said I was new in town etcetera. He gave me an address about a block away and said to ask for Mrs. Roosevelt."

"I guess she had to find something to do after Franklin died."

"It was a different Mrs. Roosevelt, not the famous one. This one was on the heavy side and had a bit of a mustache.

And it wasn't a house, it was apartments above a store."

"So what did she say?"

"She asked me if I was looking for a good time. I said maybe and asked her how much she charged. She said to come upstairs and discuss that with the party in question. That was a relief because she was no sexy tomato. She took me to a bedroom and left me there. It looked just like a regular bedroom. Not, you know, sleazy or anything. The wallpaper was kind of old though with a few stains from past roof leaks."

"Let's skip the decor. What happened?"

"Well, this girl comes in. Wearing kind of a frilly robe. It was very embarrassing because she wasn't what I had been expecting. She was young."

"How young? You mean like 12 or 13?"

"No, more like 19 to 20. I wasn't expecting someone my age. She didn't look like a prostitute at all. She was kind of pretty and looked like someone you'd meet at the roller rink or a church picnic. You know, a normal girl. Except she was wearing this kind of skimpy robe."

"What did she say?"

"She said it was $10 payable in advance. I said that was kind of steep and did she offer any discounts. She said OK, $7, but I had to use a condom and couldn't dawdle when I was done. And no kissing on the lips. I said that sounded fine. I mean why would I want to kiss a person I just met?"

"Or even someone you've been living with for ages. Go on."

"So I paid her the money and then she unbuckled my belt and pulled down my pants. No preliminaries or anything. She checked me out down there."

"Did she put two fingers under your testicles and ask you to cough?"

"Hardly. And how did you know doctors do that?"

"I have three brothers, remember? Did you pass inspection?"

"Apparently so. She handled my unit like it was a zucchini from the garden. I guess she's seen quite a few of them. Am I being too explicit here?"

"I can take it. OK, she's handling the merchandise. What did she say?"

"She said I was very impressively built."

"Oh, they all say that. Flatter his ego. Hand out the cheap compliments to build repeat business. Then what?"

"Then she asked me if it was my first time. I guess she could tell I was nervous. I said she guessed that right. You won't believe what happened next."

"Try me."

"She said I was likely to go off like a rocket, this being my first time. So she opened a drawer in the night stand and took out a familiar green can."

"The real thing or an impostor?"

"The real stuff, I checked the label. She takes a dab of Miracle Creme and rubs it on my privates. To make it less sensitive, she said. Then she put on the condom and drops her robe."

"How did she look?"

"Extremely naked. Like stark naked."

"I mean how was her body? What did she look like?"

"Very nice. Curves right where you expected them. Rosy nipples, the works. First naked girl I'd ever seen. It makes a powerful impression. Naturally I'm trying not to stare. But she looked good and she smelled good too. Still, I was pretty darn embarrassed. And then I took off the rest of my clothes and we did it."

"Could you elaborate on that?"

"She was very businesslike. We got on the bed, she moved me on top, she grabbed my pecker with her hand,

and guided me in. So there we are doing it. It really is pretty great. I can see now what all the fuss is about. About a thousand times better than going at it solo with your hand. We do it for a while and then I blast away feeling like it's the greatest roller coaster ride in the history of the world. Then we rested for a bit."

"I thought you were supposed to be out the door and not lingering."

"She must have decided she liked me. She said we could do it again if I got hard in the next two minutes. I made it by the deadline, she put on a new condom, and we were off to the races again. The second time was nice too, but your body is kind of wondering what's the point. Why are you going into extra innings when you just hit a grand-slam homer that won the seventh game of the World Series? It's like you're there for the thrills and chills, but your body is more interested in making a baby."

"That is the function of the act after all. Did you ask her why she went into that line of work?"

"Yeah, when I was putting on my clothes, but she said no personal questions. She said I seemed like a nice guy and she hoped to see me again. She said she had Tuesdays off so I should skip that night. She asked me if I had a girlfriend. I said I had one who unexpectedly blew town."

"What did she say?"

"She said yeah, she had done the same thing. Four days before the wedding. It makes you wonder: is that a regular thing with you chicks?"

"Guys do the same thing. Men are always going out for cigarettes and never coming back. Leaving the missus at the ironing board with a pack of kids screaming for dinner. Or magazines. They go out for *Popular Mechanics* and are never heard from again."

"I read that magazine. It was a gift subscription from Dot."

"No doubt to keep you from wandering. I noticed you had the same cab driver coming back."

"Yeah, I don't think they have that many working nights. He asked if I found what I was looking for. I said in a big way and thanked him for his help. He said he used to go to those places when he was in France in 1918. But now he'd rather stay home and listen to Amos 'n' Andy on the radio. It must be hell getting old."

"My mother certainly is having a difficult time of it. So do you feel better now? Have you turned the corner on your suffering?"

"I don't know. I think I may feel worse. Now I know exactly what Dot may be doing with that guy. It's kind of too painful to think about. I'll tell you one thing though."

"What's that?"

"I'll never forget Zanesville, Ohio."

Chapter 7

Parking was free at the Muskingum County Fair, and they were happy to waive the admission fee for the soldier on leave and his companion. That was it for the good news. The Magic Creem man with the backwards ears was there, but not the target of their search. He waved them over for a chat.

"Still on the prowl for Boyd, huh?"

"'Fraid so," said Wilder. "Haven't seen a sign of him."

"He's like to be around at some fair somewhere. He's got to move the goods same as me. How you enjoyin' that free can of Magic Creem I give ya?"

"Good. I noticed one of my tires had a bubble on the sidewall. I rubbed on a dollop and the bubble went away."

"Best thing in the world for tires. It really conditions the rubber. It's like a retread in a can. If you see ol' Boyd, tell him I hope he drops dead from a massive stroke."

"OK, I'll give him the message."

"I expect he'll more likely get his ass shot off by a jealous husband."

"Or boyfriend," said Verity.

They strolled up and down the aisles. The National Guard was there recruiting, but not the Marines. They checked out a flag-draped booth advertising 25 WAYS TO TELL IF YOUR NEIGHBOR IS A COMMUNIST. They watched a man demonstrate an appliance that cut an average-sized potato into a coil over 30 feet long. And another selling a magnetic device that clipped to your fuel line. It realigned the molecules in gasoline to virtually double your mileage while making carbon buildup a thing of the past. Guaranteed to work or your money cheerfully refunded.

"Yeah," said Wilder. "And try finding the guy to collect on that."

They wandered out to the midway.

"Which do you want to see, Wilder: Two Thousand Years of Chastity Belts on Live Girls or The Boy in the Iron Lung?"

"I think polio is scary enough without paying money to invade the privacy of its sufferers. Those belts might be educational."

The belts were something of a disappointment. A long table displayed a variety of grisly devices resembling iron garter belts. Gnarly chains and sharp points to discourage amorous entry. An additional 25 cents (undisclosed out front) was required to see one modeled by a live girl.

"Shall we cough up the extra half-dollar?" asked Wilder.

"You go, Wild One. I'll meet you outside. If I want to see a rigidly chaste female, I can look in the nearest mirror."

Wilder paid and got admitted to an inner tent. A bored-looking middle-aged woman was lounging in a chair. She was naked except for an arrangement of steel straps about two inches wide that extended across her waist and down around her groin. She had shaved her pubic hair but not recently. She was eating a corndog and holding a tall paper cup of what looked like beer.

"That looks uncomfortable," commented a man.

"You get used to it," she replied.

She had applied mustard to the dog, but lacked a free hand to wipe her mouth.

"How do you go to the bathroom?" inquired a youth.

"Same as you. In a toilet."

"What happens if you lose the key?" asked a woman, possibly the youth's mother.

"Then I call a locksmith."

"Do you know a fellow named Boyd Wagstaph?" asked Wilder.

"Never heard of the bum," she replied.

"He sells Miracle Creme," he elaborated.

"Hey, ask me about chastity belts, kid. That's what I'm here for. This ain't Twenty Questions. This ain't the Bureau of Missing Persons."

"How'd you get that scar?" asked the youth.

"Appendicitis, but I may get a tattoo to cover it up."

"A rose would be nice," said his mother.

"I was thinkin' more of a dragon. Or a dagger," she replied.

"Cool," said the youth. "Get one shooting fire or dripping with blood."

"How was it?" asked Verity when Wilder emerged from the tent.

"I'm glad I saw that girl naked in Zanesville. Otherwise, I might be off women for good."

Lunch was cheese-stuffed bacon horns and crusty rhubarb balls on a stick. Washed down with pink lemonade. They ate in the shade of an elm tree by an artificial duck pond.

"I'm getting discouraged, Varsity," said Wilder. "I'm thinking of packing it in."

"That's funny. I didn't think you were a quitter."

"You want to spend all summer roaming over the goddam Midwest looking for the girl who ditched me?"

"I don't think you'll be happy until you find out what happened to her, Wild Seed. You'll be hanging out there in deepest limbo. You'll be a miserable wreck. Or, you can forget all about that two-timer and make a play for me. I should warn you in advance that you are not likely to be rebuffed."

"I'm thinking we need to call home again. My mother may have heard something."

"You ready to talk to her?"

"No, but I'm sure she'd like to hear from you. You two seem to have a real rapport."

"Shall I introduce myself as her new daughter-in-law? Just to try it out on her?"

"Please don't."

Verity had another lively and animated conversation in a phone booth near the Lost Children's department. This one consumed seven quarters.

"What did she say?" asked Wilder.

"Your father loves welding. He may give up his career in screen doors."

"I doubt that. He's had that job for 23 years. He's only saying that to make me look bad. What else did she say?"

"Dot's mother got a postcard in the mail. It showed a giant tire factory in full color. Smokestacks belching away. Postmarked Akron, Ohio."

"Damn! The Summit County fair ended yesterday! We should have been there and not here! What did the postcard say?"

"Not much. She said she was having a good time and not to worry."

"Damn! Having a good time! She's not supposed to be having a good time!"

"She's young and in love, Wilder. Just not apparently with you."

"Did she mention me on the postcard?"

"No. The message was quite brief. Scrawled hurriedly. The stamp was affixed crookedly suggesting a hasty posting. Probably in between crazed lovemaking sessions in the trailer."

"Spare me the speculations, Varsity. Here we are in southern Ohio and we should have been in northern Ohio."

"There's a cute lost toddler over there, Wildness. Out of diapers and past the messiest stages. Shall we adopt him and give him a better life?"

"You mean kidnap him? I don't think so. I don't need the F.B.I. on my trail."

"I suppose you want to grow your own. That's easy for a guy to say. All you have to do is have a pleasurable bodily convulsion and you're done. Piece of cake for you. Thank God they invented baby formulas to eliminate that nasty nursing business. I for one am *not* a cow."

"What did you say, Varsity? I wasn't listening."

"Nothing, dear. Are you ready to hit the road?"

"Let's roll."

They stopped in Mt. Vernon, Ohio because Wilder had another brainwave. He pulled into a Flying A gas station and parked by the phone booth.

"OK, Varsity, I want you to call a girl named Amy Hochkiss. She's Dot's best friend. I phoned her when I was in Erie, and she claimed she was totally in the dark. But she might have been lying. Tell her you're from a nursing school and you're trying to get in touch with Dolores Bateman. Tell her she's been awarded a full scholarship and you need to contact her right away."

"What nursing school?"

"I don't know. Make something up."

"What will you give me for placing this deceptive call?"

"I don't know. What do you want?"

"How about a kiss on the lips? Lasting at least two minutes."

"Fine. Whatever."

"A full embrace and kissing like you mean it."

"OK, it's a deal. Now can you make the call?"

"All right. I'll give it a shot."

Verity returned to the car a few minutes later.

"I talked to Amy. What a ditz. I told her I was from the Albert Schweitzer School of Nursing and Cosmetology. She sounded impressed. No, she doesn't have Dot's address, but she just received an Akron postcard too. Sounds like everyone got one except you. This one showed some boys racing soapbox derby cars. The message was brief. Dot wrote that she was having a good time and making 78 cents an hour. Amy also wants to be a nurse. I said we still had some scholarships available. I told her to send a transcript of her high-school grades and an essay entitled 'Why I Want To Nurse Really Sick People' to Box 1931, Grand Central Station, New York, New York."

"Is that your post office box?"

"No, but I imagine it's somebody's."

"Why did you specify 1931?"

"First number that came to mind. It's the year of my birth."

"Same here. Seventy-eight cents an hour, huh? That's possibly useful information."

"How so?"

"If they were lovers, would he be paying her that much?"

"Hey, partner, where I come from them's starvation wages."

"OK, would she be making it with the guy if he was paying her so poorly?"

"I leave that for you to decide. If you want to dance on the head of that pin, be my guest. Are you ready to pucker up?"

"OK, but let's not go overboard."

"Meaning what?"

"No tongue."

They embraced on the front seat and went at it. The clinch reached the two-minute mark and continued on. A Flying A employee in soiled coveralls tapped on the window and told them to knock it off, so they did.

"How was it?" asked Verity.

"Not bad," he conceded. "I can see you've had some practice. And you're not as bony as I thought."

A few miles north of town they pulled into Wayne Lake Campground, named for mad Anthony Wayne, conqueror of the Ohio Indian tribes, not John Wayne the actor. Checking in, Wilder signed the guest register as he always did Mr. and Mrs. Wilder S. Flint.

"Wilder S. Flint," said the elderly manager. "I just encountered that name. Recently, in fact. Now where did I hear that name?"

"Did you have some folks staying here in a Spartan trailer?" Wilder asked eagerly. "Pulled by a Cadillac. Did a pretty blonde girl mention my name?"

"No, I don't recall any Spartans or pretty blonds. No, it was in regards to something else. Wilder S. Flint, yes, that was the name. No mistaking that moniker. Have you been in the news lately, young man?"

"Uh, no. I don't think so."

"Well, I'll think of it. I have quite a remarkable memory. That will be one dollar for one night."

Wilder was worried when they pulled into their assigned camping spot.

"It must be in the newspapers, Varsity. Or on the radio. They must be broadcasting my garage mishap all over the goddam state!"

"You're sounding paranoid, Wild Bird. Why would anyone care about a minor incident of vandalism in another state? I'm practically a journalist myself. Believe me, no reporter gives a hoot about your petty crimes."

"Then how did that man hear about me?"

"There must be some other Wilder S. Flint out there. The Manhattan phone book lists four Verity Warrens, all of whom are probably having a more fulfilling life than this one. Are you going swimming in that lake?"

"I think I will. I might as well have a few hours of pleasure before they haul me off to jail. Did you pack a bathing suit in your duffel?"

"I did. Now put up the tent so I have a place to change."

Like many campgrounds they encountered, this one had started out as a farm. The "lake" was a cow pond that had been enlarged by building up the earthen berm. The tractor in the barn now pulled a grass mower instead of a disc plow. Trees had been planted here and there to interrupt the agricultural vistas, but they had many years to grow before they provided any useful shade. Arrayed on the opposite side of the lake from the trailers were a half-dozen prefab cabins, all painted white with green trim.

Wilder changed in the car. He inspected his companion when she emerged from the tent.

"Wow, Varsity. You look damn good."

"Don't sound so surprised," she replied, adjusting her straps. "I've been told my shape is not entirely devoid of interest. I may not have Mae West's figure, but at least I'll never be tripping over my tits. You should try to even out that tan, Wildness. You look like a two-tone Ford."

While they swam, Wilder listened for the sound of approaching sheriffs' cars. But no sirens were heard.

The next morning at breakfast Verity announced that she'd had an epiphany.

"Is that another female condition I should know about?" asked Wilder.

"Listen up, buddy. We don't have to drive all over this state to find Dot the Bounder."

"We don't?"

"No. Here's what you do: You phone all the fairs open-ing this week. You say you're trying to reach an exhibitor named Boyd Wagstaph. You say it's an emergency. His twin brother is deathly ill and needs a transfusion, but Boyd is the only one whose blood is a perfect match."

"Does Boyd have a twin brother?"

"That is immaterial. This call will elicit one of two re-sponses: 'We're sorry, no Boyd Wagstaph is registered at this fair.' Or, 'Hang on, sir, we'll go get him.'"

"Jesus, Varsity, that sounds like it might work."

"I know. We sit tight right here. If we get a confirmation, off we go."

"Hell, I don't have to stay here. I can go back to Erie and call from home!"

"And risk having your mother confiscate the car keys?"

"Oh, right. I forgot about that."

"This area is ideal, being near the center of the state. We can drive in any direction from here. And I was talking to the manager last night, Wildness. They rent out those cute cabins for only $12 a week."

"Why would we want to rent a cabin?"

"Because I'm sick of that tent. It and everything in it is soaking wet by morning. And nothing ever dries out. And the forecast calls for rain this week. They were having severe thunderstorms in Indiana yesterday."

"I don't know, Varsity. Twelve dollars is a lot of money. What if we're only here a day or two?"

"I'll pay half, Wilder. We rent the cabin or it's bye-bye Verity. I'll be off to dryer climes."

"Oh, all right."

"It's the fellow's wife who is in charge of the cabins. He implied that she's a bit more of a stickler than he is."

"Meaning what?"

"Meaning we need to display wedding rings."

"I'm not marrying you, Varsity. I'm 1A and otherwise taken."

"Don't be an ass. I'm not suggesting that. We can go into town and buy me a fake ring at Woolworth's. You can turn your gaudy high-school ring around so only the thin part of the band shows. It can pass for a wedding ring."

"I paid $35 for this ring. It's genuine 14k gold."

"I suppose they told you that big lump of faceted blue glass was a sapphire?"

"No, the order form said it was a semi-precious gem."

"No doubt. With an emphasis on *semi.*"

"I think we should make the calls before we rent the cabin. But I'm not sure I have enough quarters."

"We'll get a roll of them at a bank while we're in town. And get some groceries too. It's going to be fun, Wildest."

"Being reunited with Dot?"

"No, sharing that cozy lake side cabin."

In Woolworth's they inspected the 29-cent rings and the 59-cent rings. Wilder splurged and went for the luxury look. Verity slipped it on her finger as they left the store.

"How does it look, honey?" she asked, displaying the sparkler on her left hand.

"It looks like you're married all right–to a really cheap bastard."

"I'll keep my hand in motion so no one gets a close look at it. And you do the same."

Wilder took his notebook and roll of quarters into a phone booth while Verity shopped at an A&P. They met up back at the car. Wilder looked discouraged.

"I called three fairs and he's not registered at any of them."

"They must be at some other kind of festival this week. Or still on their honeymoon."

"Please, Varsity, don't say things like that. I really can't take it."

"Sorry, honey. I'll try to be like you and ignore reality."

The manager's name was Mrs. Murchforble. She was a vision of rural rectitude in a flowery Sears house dress, crepe-soled shoes, hair net, and wire-rimmed glasses.

"You folks look awfully young to be married," she observed, unlocking the door to Cabin Three. It was a one-room square box, 16-feet on a side, with exposed wooden studs and a compact bathroom grafted onto the back. The toilet tank was missing its lid and the metal shower was losing a battle against rust.

"We met when we were four," said Verity, waving her hands about. "He proposed when we were six, but I told him I was too young to commit."

No smile from the landlady. The cabin smelled musty. It was furnished sparely to achieve a look of grimness. One corner was devoted to a spartan kitchenette.

"No bed, huh?" said Wilder.

Mrs. Murchforble opened double closet doors.

"It's a Murphy bed. It came with springs to ease it on down, but larcenous tenants have made off with them over the years. Don't ask me what they do with them. So you have to be careful lowering the bed. You have to be ready to take its full weight. But you look like a strong young man. I never rent to women couples for this and other obvious reasons."

"Any chance we could also get a roll-away cot?" he asked.

"I thought you said there were only two people. I can't have people sneaking in guests who aren't registered."

"There's only the two of us," said Verity. "My husband can be a restless sleeper. I've been known to kick him out of bed."

"Sorry, no cots are provided. You should have asked him about his sleeping habits before you married him."

"Right," she replied. "I'll keep that in mind for the next time."

Their hostess showed them where to put a quarter into a slot if they wanted hot water for the shower. And where to put a dime in the radio to activate it.

"If the radio stops, it's not broken. It means your time is up. So don't go thumping on the cabinet. And you will be charged for any and all cigarette burns."

"Neither of us smokes," said Verity, continuing the hand waving.

"You look kind of nervous, Mrs. Flint," she said. "Is the honeymoon not going well? Is he forcing himself on you?"

"No, everything's fine," Verity replied, still gesturing exuberantly. "We couldn't be happier."

Chapter 8

The rain arrived while Verity was making dinner.

"Look at it pour, Wildest. It's coming down in buckets. Our tent would have been instantly swamped. We might have drowned like rats in that monsoon."

"We could have sat in the car until it blows over."

"But you wouldn't be dining on a delicious home-cooked dinner."

"Aren't we having spaghetti out of a can?"

"True, but I'm making the salad from scratch, assuming I can find a knife capable of cutting this carrot. And we're going to have fresh-brewed coffee. And Ann Page lemon cake for dessert. You are one lucky fellow."

"I guess. Shall I put a dime in the radio?"

"Please do, darling."

Wilder found a station out of Columbus playing dance music.

"That's nice," said Verity.

"I think it's really chintzy that they ding us to the play the radio. It's a wonder they haven't put a coin slot on the bathroom door."

"Don't give them any ideas. Oh dear, these meatballs are much smaller than they appear on the label of the can."

"That's no surprise. Life is full of disappointments."

"Realizing that is a sign of your developing maturity, Wild One. We seldom get everything we want."

"I seldom get anything I want."

"That's not exactly true, honey. There, I believe dinner is served."

Dinner arrived on mismatched plates. Every item in the kitchenette represented the absolute irreducible that no one could possibly want to steal.

The radio cut out during dessert. Wilder sighed and got up to insert another dime. Phil Spitalny and his All-girl Orchestra resumed their rumba.

"I may have another piece of that cake," he said.

"Let me cut it for you, honey."

Verity carved off another slab with the dull knife and put it on his plate.

"That was sure smart of you figuring out how to call those fairs, Varsity. You saved us hundreds of miles of needless driving."

"That fattening fair food and those dismal sideshows were beginning to pall. More coffee, hon?"

"I don't mind if I do."

The downpour went on. The lights flickered a few times, but the power didn't go out. Wilder did the dishes while Verity relaxed on the oak divan, apparently designed for maximum discomfort in any seating position.

"It takes living in a tent for a person to appreciate the comforts of civilization," she remarked, moving over to a straight-back chair with a bad wobble.

"I guess I can sleep in the car tonight," said Wilder, hanging up the threadbare dish towel.

"You'll do nothing of the sort. That Murphy bed is plenty wide enough for two."

"I didn't bring any pajamas."

"You can sleep in your underwear. I won't mind. You don't have anything that I haven't seen plenty of times before."

"Yes, but you haven't seen my particular version of it."

"We'll turn out the lights if you're shy. You can stay on your side of the bed and I'll stay on mine. Nothing untoward will transpire. All we'll do is sleep. We're adults. We can exercise restraint."

"I'm glad you feel that way. I think my air mattress has a slow leak. It wants to bottom out in the middle of the night."

Verity went to the bathroom first. While she was gone, Wilder dealt with the bed. It was built for the ages of stout steel, and the lack of counter-balancing springs offered a true test of his strength. The bed thudded down all made up with sheets, blanket, and two thin pillows. Wilder gave it a test sit. Not as much sag as he'd been expecting.

Verity emerged wearing a demure nightgown.

"How's the bed?" she asked.

"Better than I expected. It's built like a tank. If it got away from you, it could kill someone."

Then it was Wilder's turn to use the facilities. He emerged in T-shirt and jockey shorts. He darted over to the bed and slithered between the sheets.

"This is not bad," he said. "Shall I turn off the light?"

"Oh, let's leave it on for a bit. Are you sleepy?"

"No, I should have skipped that second cup of coffee. He rolled onto his side and faced her. She smiled back at him."

"Don't smile like that."

"Why not?"

"Because you look too cute."

"Sorry. That was not my intention. I like your eyes; have I mentioned that lately?"

"Yours aren't bad either. What are they, brown?"

"Sort of hazel in some light. You have a nice face too. You wear your ring to bed, huh?

"I thought I'd better. In case of midnight inspections by that nosy old gal. How's your ring working out?"

"It hasn't turned my finger green yet."

Wilder fluffed up his pillow, then resumed his position. Verity was still smiling at him.

"You could give me a good-night kiss," she suggested.

"OK, I'll kiss you. But nothing else is going to happen."

"Of course. I understand."

He leaned over and their lips met. They moved a bit closer and he put his arms around her. They kissed again.

"That was pretty swell," she said.

"We could do it some more."

"We could. A little kissing never got anyone in trouble."

The next kiss went on for quite some time.

"I'm getting a little warm," she said. "You could unbutton my nightgown a bit."

"OK, but nothing else is going to happen."

"Certainly. Nothing else. We're absolutely firm on that point."

Wilder undid quite a few of her buttons. They kissed again and he felt compelled to place a hand on her warm breast. A finger found its way to a nipple and began to caress it softly.

"You could take off that T-shirt if you're warm," she said.

"OK, but I'm not taking off anything else."

"Right. We both need to exercise some restraint here."

Wilder removed his shirt and tossed it across the room. They resumed their previous activities. Verity shifted her hip for more contact with his torso and its firm promontory.

"You could touch me with your hand," she suggested. "I'm not wearing anything down there. Just a gentle touch might be nice."

"OK, but we're stopping at that."

"Good idea. I understand."

Wilder slid down his hand, and making his way under

her nightgown, found her warm wetness. He began to stroke very lightly. She kissed him and moaned softly.

"Shall I remove my nightgown?" she asked.

"OK, it's kind of getting in the way."

"Why don't you take off your shorts too? I'd like to feel you against me."

"All right. But we're stopping there."

"Good. We're both in agreement on that."

All the clothing impediments got tossed from the bed. They converged in a full naked embrace.

"Would you be offended if I said you were impressively built?" she asked, grasping him with a firm grip.

"I don't mind. I wouldn't do too much of that or the show's going to be over fast."

"It's hard to resist though. Shall I rub just the tip?"

"No, that'll get you in trouble just as fast."

"Do you mind if I lift up the covers and look at it?"

"I guess not. We've come this far. You might as well see what's what."

"It's considerably bigger than what my little brother was exhibiting when I used to give him baths."

"Things tend to grow during puberty."

"No wonder boys that age act so strange. It's awfully inflamed looking. Does it hurt?"

"Quite the contrary. It's having a very good time."

"Mine is too. We could put them together and see what happens."

"Do you still have those condoms in your duffel?"

"I do. But I also secreted a couple under my pillow while you were in the bathroom."

"We need to clear up where we stand if we do this."

"Well, assuming you're up to the task, I expect no longer to be a virgin."

"You're not thinking this is a commitment to marry you?"

"I live in the 20th century, Wildness. You're the one living in the 18th century. We're two people having a good time in bed. No crime is being committed here. No one is here to notarize our signatures on the dotted line. How about you put on the rubber while I watch? This is supposed to be educational after all."

Wilder demonstrated that aspect of the procedure.

"It looks pretty silly now. And remarkably obscene."

"Shall we give it a whirl?"

"OK, but let's take it slow."

They took it slow but considerable force was required. Union happened at last, and Wilder began to move slowly.

"How's that?" he asked.

"Probably not as bad as actual childbirth."

"Should I stop?"

"No, it's feeling kind of nice now."

They continued on until she felt him quaking inside her. He withdrew and lay beside her.

"Not to over-intellectualize here, Wild One, but this sex business is pretty weird. Having another person inside you: that's a whole new concept in social intercourse."

"It feels kind of natural to me."

"Is that it for tonight's show?"

"We could do it again if you like. I'd need a while to regroup."

"How does it work? Do you will yourself to get hard again?"

"No, it's kind of indirect. We do sexy things and it gets in the mood on its own."

They did that and the result was as predicted. This time Verity put on the condom. They went for round two, which lasted much longer. When Wilder finished, Verity asked him to do her with his hand.

"OK, if you show me how."

She guided him to the spot and he did what she suggested. Moments later he felt her moving in ecstatic quivers.

Eventually, the light got switched off and they fell asleep. The rain slowed to a steady drizzle. For the first time in weeks Wilder slept through the night. A knock on the door woke them early in the morning. Wilder wrapped Verity's nightgown around him and opened the door a crack.

"Good morning," said Mr. Murchfoble. "I remembered where I saw your name. Here's the classified section of the Columbus paper. I've circled the ad. Quite a storm, huh? More predicted for today. Is that your nightgown?"

"No, I borrowed it from, uh, my wife."

"I hope it was with her consent. My wife seems to think you're something of a brute."

"I picked it up from where she dropped it on the floor. Everything's fine here."

"Glad to hear it. Well, I'll be off. I don't need the paper back."

"What a couple of busybodies!" exclaimed Verity from the bed. "What's in that paper?"

The circled ad was in the Personal Announcements section. It read: "Wilder S. Flint. Call home collect. Mom."

"How did she know I was in the Columbus area?" asked Wilder.

"I doubt if she did. She's probably put ads in all the major Ohio newspapers."

"What a waste of money! And with my father out on strike."

"She's worried about you, honey. It's time you bit the bullet and called her."

"She's only going to give me grief."

"That's what mothers are for, darling. You should meet mine to experience a real practitioner of the art. How about putting a quarter in the slot so I can take a shower?"

Wilder did so and realized too late that he had spent his lucky red-painted quarter.

"Damn!" he exclaimed.

"What's the matter?"

"Oh, nothing. It wasn't doing me much good anyway."

"What wasn't?"

"That quarter I just put in the slot."

"Are you OK?"

"I'm fine."

"Then come over here and let's cuddle until the water's warm."

He returned to the bed and they embraced.

"How did you sleep?" she asked.

"Fine. No problems."

"I've worked my magic on you."

"That was kind of premeditated of you, Varsity. Stashing those condoms under your pillow."

"I only did it for my protection. In case the brute I was bunking with forced himself on me."

"I'm supposed to be looking for the girl I love. And now in less than a week I've slept with two different girls. That doesn't say much for my sincerity."

"Feeling guilty, huh? Well, you shouldn't. You're taking the required steps to get over that Bounder. There is nothing she could offer you that you weren't getting in spades last night."

"It's still raining. I guess I won't be washing any windows today."

"Good. You can stay here and be nice to me."

"We might get bored. There's not much to do in this cabin."

"We'll think of something."

They showered, ate a leisurely breakfast, then retired to the bed. A few hours later Wilder said, "I guess I should call her. I might have got a letter from the draft board."

"We could drive into Mt. Vernon. Have a look around. Call your mother. Then pick up some things for dinner."

Many roads converged in a circle in the center of Mt. Vernon; its colonial architecture reminded Verity of villages back in Connecticut. Towering over the small park enclosed by the circle was a granite memorial. All four sides of its base were carved with inscriptions commemorating the men of Knox County who had given their lives for the Union cause during the Civil War.

"I wonder how many of those guys were draftees," said Wilder, who had turned up the collar of his poplin jacket against the drizzle.

"Back then if you had the money, you could buy your way out of the draft. How fair was that? As I recall, a good percentage of the men who fought on both sides were volunteers."

They found a phone booth and Wilder made the collect call while Verity waited under a nearby store awning.

"Did she read you the riot act?" she asked, when he had hung up.

"Not as bad as I expected. She mostly wanted to know if I was OK and when I was coming back. My dad's still in New Philadelphia learning to weld, so she's all by herself. I told her to cancel those ads and I'd reimburse the cost."

"Did you mention my name?"

"Not hardly. She did say some nice friend of Dot's has been phoning her long distance. Someone Dot's mother had never heard of. Also she said Dot's dad took leave from his job and is in Ohio looking for her too. He's a milkman. Dot's mom is having to deliver his route. She's been getting the orders mixed up. Dieters are having to cope with quarts of heavy cream."

"That girl sure has everyone in an uproar."

"You're AWOL too, Varsity. Your dad might have detectives and the state police looking for you. He might be calling in some favors from Al Jolson and his crowd. They might have your photo posted in every Howard Johnson's in the country."

"Hey, I sent them that postcard. What more do they want?"

"Now you're shacking up with some guy in a tawdry love nest."

"And he's a fugitive from justice to boot. So what do you want for dinner, honey?"

"I don't know. Surprise me."

After they got back to the cabin, Wilder fell silent. He sat down in an unnatural position on the oak settee lost in thought. Verity hoped he was thinking about her.

"What's up, Wildman?"

"It's the brakes of my car. I think they're getting worse."

"I noticed you've been tugging on the emergency brake now when you stop."

"I think I need to get them looked at. Bad steering and no brakes make us a hazard on the highway."

"You could take it to a garage and get an estimate. If it's too much money, you could buy the parts and do it yourself."

"I could if I had any tools and knew what I was doing. Brake work is not really a job for your under-tooled amateur."

"We could ask Mr. Murchfoble if he knows any good mechanics who work cheap."

"That's an idea. Both he and his wife look like they know how to squeeze a nickel. I wonder if they need any work done around here. I need to earn some quick bucks."

"I can float you a loan from my reserves."

"How much cash are you carrying anyway?"

"Enough to get by."

"Great. Making you even more of a target when you're out there hitchhiking."

"I'm not doing that now, honey. I'm making you another delicious dinner."

"Which is what?"

"Ann Page Oyster stew with Ann Page biscuits. With the rest of her lemon cake for dessert."

"I should skip the middleman and just shack up with Ann Page."

"Or Betty Crocker, hon. I hear she's a tigress in bed. Or there's Aunt Jemima if miscegenation is your style."

By next morning the rain had stopped, but the gray clouds lingered on. All the tent campers had fled, and the remaining trailer residents appeared discouraged and lethargic. Wilder found Mr. Murchfoble in the office where he was reading the *Columbus Dispatch*. To pass the time he reads every word in that paper (including the classified ads) every day. Wilder found that hard to believe.

"You mean you read all the ads in the 'Help Wanted - Colored Female' category?" he asked.

"I sure do. If I ever want to hire a colored maid or laundry gal, I'll know what the going rate is. You won't find me overpaying my help."

Mr. Murchfoble had no work for Wilder (his wife discouraged such entanglements with tenants), but he said his handyman Gustavus did car repairs on the side.

With his long white beard and unkempt hair Gustavus looked like a Biblical prophet in bib overalls. He had once been a prosperous farmer in Kansas, but had lost the farm and his wife in the Dust Bowl calamity. He said the Plymouth had a leaky master cylinder and two leaky wheel cylinders. He offered to hone the cylinders, replace the seals, and flush the system for $10 plus parts and one home-cooked dinner.

"My wife isn't much of a cook," said Wilder. "She mostly opens cans and heats up the contents."

"That so, huh? Why'd you marry her?"

"Well, I guess I loved her."

"Loved gettin' her in the bedroom you mean. You musta forgot a man spends a lot more of his life sittin' at the dinner table than workin' out his kinks on a mattress." He slid his tobacco chaw to the other side of his mouth and spat a brown liquid into the grass. "We'll make it a straight $12 cash for the labor."

Gustavus refused any estimate for the wobbly front end, believing that part of the car was beyond hope. He said every car when it left the factory faced its ultimate date with the junk yard and the Plymouth was "chugging along" well past its time.

Wilder thought of one more question. "Do you offer any sort of guarantee on your work?"

"I guarantee you'll get yourself kilt fast if you don't get those brakes mended."

Wilder agreed to his terms and asked when the job would be completed.

"Tomorrow probably. Next week, maybe. Never if I drop dead today."

"By tomorrow would be great. I need the car for my work."

"I'll see what I can do."

Chapter 9

By the end of the week the sun had reappeared, the Plymouth's hemorrhaging of brake fluid had ceased, Wilder had earned $23 washing windows, and they were down to their last condom. Oral sex had been experimented with and added to the nightly menu. They were merging their persons with an enthusiasm that showed no signs of abating. But now a page of the calendar had turned and September loomed directly ahead.

"August in Ohio," sighed Verity, climbing into the Plymouth. "You can cut the humidity with a machete. Did I tell you my father has air conditioning in his Buick?"

"Not good to subject the body to those extremes of hot and cold," said Wilder, starting the engine. "It's best just to roll down a window."

"Have you ever ridden in an air-conditioned car?"

"Well, no. But at the store I used to go in and out of the walk-in freezer."

"And did you die from that experience? Did you catch pneumonia? Did the sudden temperature changes drive you insane?"

"Air conditioning puts an unnecessary drag on the motor. Your gas mileage suffers. A.C. will never catch on. It's just a gimmick they slap into luxury cars to jack up the price."

"It also happens to be wonderful on a hot day. You should try it before you dismiss it."

"Once you've lived through a few winters in Erie, you'll never mind the heat."

"I don't expect to be doing that, Wildness."

"I know. I was just talking about life there in general."

Their first stop in Mt. Vernon was the bank. Wilder invested in more rolls of quarters and dimes to feed the many coin slots they faced daily. Down Main Street at a drug store Wilder worked up the nerve to ask the clerk for a dozen condoms. Verity had suggested he buy two dozen, but he wasn't sure they'd be together that long. And he didn't want to look like a sex fiend to the druggist. While she stocked up at the A&P, Wilder phoned the county fairs that had just opened. Not one had an exhibitor named Wagstaph.

"That snake must know I'm looking for him," said Wilder on the drive back. "That's why he's lying low."

"I saw a flyer in the window of the A&P, Wild One. There's a dance in town tomorrow night. The band is coming all the way down from Cleveland."

"A dance, huh? I guess you're determined to be there."

"Yes, and I'm dragging you with me."

"I didn't pack my fancy-evenings-on-the-town wardrobe."

"We'll manage. You can wear your jacket. We'll scrounge up a tie from somewhere."

After sex Wilder was inclined to fall asleep, but Verity often wished to talk. That night she had more on her mind.

"Wilder, honey, I've been thinking about your absent Dolores."

"What about her?" he yawned.

"You say she was saving herself for marriage. Are you aware girls sometimes say that because they are both ignorant about birth control and terrified of getting pregnant? Or they don't trust the boy to use protection?"

"I think she was just saving herself for marriage."

"So you claim. So how far along did you get? Did you get your hand under her bra?"

"I guess so. A few times. It was a struggle."

"How about between her legs?"

"Nope. Never."

"Did you try?"

"Jesus, Varsity, that's kind of personal."

"So you did try. OK. Did she ever touch your penis?"

"You mean bare hand on bare pecker?"

"I'm not getting the distinction. Was she squeamish? Would she only touch you while wearing rubber gloves? Or was she like a debutante and never removed her white gloves?"

"She never touched my dick. Except while we were making out I might get a bit excited down there. And moving about she might have brushed against me accidentally."

"It wasn't accidental, believe me. She was checking things out. She was seeing if she was turning you on."

"You think?"

"Of course. So you'd make out, you'd get totally frustrated, and then what did you do? Did you go home and masturbate?"

"Yeah, sure. What else? Otherwise, you die of blue balls."

"I suppose all guys do that?"

"Pretty much."

"Do you find our transition odd? That we've gone from no sex at all to sex all the time?"

"Odd like how? Like we're perverts or degenerates?"

"No, just that humans are so adaptable. And then when you dump me on the highway, we'll go back to no sex at all. Will you miss it?"

"Sure I will. I'll miss you too."

"Will you miss me for the sex or otherwise?"

"Well, I probably won't miss your cooking. But I'll miss everything else about you."

"Will you miss me as much as you've been missing Dot?"

"I don't know. Probably. I guess so."

"So you may be *twice* as miserable as you were before?"

"Yeah, thanks for reminding me."

"I'll miss you, love. I'll miss having you inside me. I don't know how I'll get along without you."

"I'm 1A, Varsity. I'm going away soon for two years. There's nothing I can do about that."

"Guys get out of the draft. There are ways."

"I'm not like that. I'll go serve my country. I'll do my duty. Hell, I may come out of the services knowing what I want to do with my life."

"Or not come back at all. Things are looking bad with the Russians in Germany. And people are worried about Korea too."

"I'll fight if I have to. But the Ruuskies backed down. They called off their blockade of Berlin. I expect everyone's sick of war now. I hear they killed 50 million in the last one. That ought to hold 'em for a while. I'll spend two years mowing the grass at some army post and that will be that."

"Do you ever think you'd be better off if you'd never met Dot and me?"

"No way."

"Why not? You wouldn't be so miserable."

"True. But guys need to be with girls. Life is no fun without them."

"Yeah. It's the same for us. I don't see how single people cope."

"They drink. They smoke. They work at their jobs. They have hobbies."

Verity thought it over. "Or they have religion like nuns and priests."

No reply from Wilder. He was asleep.

Having no shame, Verity borrowed a tie from Gustavus, who lived in squalor in the converted tack room of the Wayne Lake barn. The cravat was narrower than the current style and had been given away years ago as an advertising premium by the makers of agricultural windmills. It was of red imitation silk dotted with whirling blades rendered in brilliant yellow. It was threadbare in spots and not scrupulously clean. Wilder put it on, but said it would stop traffic in the streets and make him the object of ridicule.

"People won't notice you, Wild Dog," said Verity, slipping into a stylish sheath dress that had emerged from her duffel. "No one cares what guys wear. How do I look?"

"Very fetching. People will wonder who is that sophisticated cutie and why is she dancing with that hayseed?"

"That is my intention, of course." She daubed on some perfume (Indiscret by Lucien Lelong) from her duffel and applied assorted cosmetics. Dangling earrings completed the look. Wilder marveled at the transformation.

"Damn, Varsity, you look great naked and very fine made up for town."

"I know. It's only the times in between that I'm invisible to men."

"You smell good too. Did some guy give you that perfume?"

"I wish. It was a going-away present I liberated from my mother's vanity table. Come closer, honey."

"Why?"

"Just as an experiment I want to try a little mascara on your sexy baby blues."

"No way."

"Please! It's just to see what it looks like. You can wash it off if you don't like it."

Wilder reluctantly let her darken his eyelashes with her mascara brush.

"A vast improvement!" she exclaimed. "Don't rub it off! I promise you, no one's going to notice that little bit of make-up. And it makes such a world of difference."

"I can't go out looking like this."

"You will if you love me. With your new movie-star eyes nobody's going to notice that ratty old tie."

They went to the dance with a young couple from Cabin Five. For the past several days the guys had been ignoring each other as men do, but the girls had started chatting in the laundry building. Tom and Wilder rode in the front seat of Tom's '46 Olds 88, while Verity and Ruth Edna occupied the back seat.

"Tom honey," said Ruth Edna, "Wilder here is a window washer."

"Not professionally," said Wilder. "I've been doing it for gas money."

"We had to leave West Virginia abruptly," explained Verity. "My husband's wanted there on a major vandalism charge."

"It was just an accident," said Wilder. "The garage was undermined by bugs. What do you do, Tom?"

"I work for my dad's bail bonds agency. So did you break bail, Wilder? Is there a bondsman looking for you?"

"The cops didn't grab him," said Verity. "We skipped town right away. The sole witness disappeared under mysterious circumstances."

"That is totally untrue," said Wilder. "Verity likes to exaggerate. It was a minor incident. We're on vacation and ran a little short of funds. That's why I washed a few windows."

"Wilder has a serious gambling addiction," said Verity. "I expect he'll lose me in a poker game someday. I'll be transferred like chattel to some cigar-smoking cardsharp. The things you find out after you tie the knot. I suppose you've had a few surprises yourself, Ruth Edna."

"Oh dear, yes. Tom has a major problem with gas. He's worse than this old coon dog we used to have."

"Just adjusting to your strenuous cuisine, sweetheart," said Tom, glancing at her in his rear-view mirror. His look was not laden with marital love.

"My Wilder is just the opposite," said Verity. "He had a very repressed childhood. He'd rather explode than commit a digestive faux pas. And anal retentive! If he visits the can once a month I'm amazed."

"Verity likes to tease," said Wilder. "Don't believe a word she says."

"Tom has amazingly hairless legs," continued Ruth Edna. "I'm so jealous. And shapely too. He should insure them for a million dollars like Betty Grable. If you dolled him up in a pair of nylons and a short skirt, I swear he'd put the rest of us girls to shame."

"Is he self-conscious about that?" asked Verity. "You know a little Miracle Creme applied to the skin can encourage hair growth. It's worked wonders on Wilder."

"He uses it on his legs, dear?" asked Ruth Edna.

"Mostly on the groin region. He had some issues down there. But I told him I loved him just the same."

"Men are so much more vain that we are!" exclaimed Ruth Edna.

"Isn't that the truth, sister," said Verity. "You don't know what vanity is until you've seen my Wilder in front of a mirror."

"I know," said Ruth Edna. "They do love to strut and preen!"

Verity had been hoping for Negro musicians, but the band turned out to be a quintet of pudgy white guys in matching green blazers trimmed in gold. Two of them were unpacking accordions, which she took as an ominous sign.

"My God," said Tom. "It's Big Al Radwanski. I saw them in Steubenville last fall. They're great."

"Who?" said Verity.

"Big Al Radwanski and the Barber Poles," said Tom. "You know, the Midwest's hottest polka band. Al and the two guys on clarinet and saxophone started out as barbers."

A waitress brought four mugs of beer to their table; Wilder paid.

Big Al's glittering accordion shot blinding flashes of light across the audience. He grabbed the microphone, yelled "Cześć wszystkim!" and his fingers flew across the keyboard. A great roar of approval rose from the crowd. Soon the area in front of the bandstand was jammed with dancing Mt. Vernonites, including Tom and Ruth Edna.

"Apparently that's the polka, Wild One," said Verity. "Bouncy beat, huh? Shall we try it?"

"I'm not speaking to you."

"OK, I'll be good. No more teasing. I promise. Come on, honey, let's dance."

"I don't know how to dance a polka."

"Neither do I, so we're even. But who cares? Let's give it a shot."

They danced many polkas, plus some polonaises and mazurkas. Wilder relaxed and began to have a good time. The beer helped. They switched partners and he danced with Ruth Edna, who whispered in his ear, "Don't worry, hon. You're the cutest guy in the place. And so bold to wear a little make-up. I wish my Tom was that brave."

Wilder immediately excused himself to go to the men's room, where he washed his face.

The dance was supposed to end at midnight, but the crowd wouldn't let Big Al go. Finally he said, "Last song, folks! It's a long drive back to Cleveland. And we don't want to be late for mass tomorrow!"

Ruth Edna, who knew how to nurse a beer, took over the wheel for the drive back to the campground. It was a warm night, so they rode with all the windows rolled down. The wind that ruffled their hair smelled like new-mown hay. Fireflies, plentiful in Ohio after dark, had all gone to bed.

"Wow, it gets dark here," said Verity, leaning out her window. "You don't see stars like that back east."

"Speaking of stars," said Wilder. "Verity's dad has a golf date tomorrow with Al Jolson."

"Al Jolson, the singer?" asked Tom.

"The one and only," said Wilder.

"That's amazing," said their driver. "I wonder if he knows Vaughn Monroe."

"Who?" said Wilder.

"You know, Vaughn Monroe," she replied. "He has that big hit now 'Ghost Riders in the Sky.' He's from Akron."

"And Doris Day," said Tom, "she's from Cincinnati." He began to sing, "Gonna take a sentimental journey. Gonna take your clothes off too."

"Oh you, hush up," said Ruth Edna, "And Clark Gable, he's from Cadiz, Ohio. They mine coal there. They have a little house in the center of town made entirely from coal."

"Do they heat it with gas?" asked Wilder.

Ruth Edna nearly ran off the road she laughed so hard at that one.

"Not to mention Thomas Edison," said Tom. "he was from Milan, Ohio."

"Did he have any hit records?" asked Verity.

"He only invented the phonograph!" said Ruth Edna. "Nobody would have any hit records if it wasn't for Ohio."

"And Clark Gable might still be building tires in Akron if Edison hadn't invented movies," said Tom.

"Clark Gable worked in a rubber factory?" said Wilder. "I didn't know that."

"He worked there for a time," said Ruth Edna, "but he decided he'd rather get paid the big money chasing Joan Crawford in Hollywood."

"Nice work if you can get it," said Tom.

"Is Joan Crawford from Ohio?" asked Verity.

"I think she might be from Texas," said Ruth Ann. "Of course, the Gish sisters are from Springfield. Lillian and Dorothy. And Roy Rogers was born down near Cincinnati."

"Is he married to Ginger Rogers?" asked Verity.

"Heavens no!" exclaimed Ruth Edna. "He's married to Dale Evans. I thought everyone knew that. Burgess Meredith and Margaret Hamilton are both from Cleveland."

"Is she that weepy kid that cries in all her movies?" asked Wilder.

"That's Margaret O'Brien," said Ruth Edna. "Margaret Hamilton played the Wicked Witch of the West in the 'Wizard of Oz.' I'm kind of annoyed that my favorite actress is from Iowa."

"Who's that?" asked Verity.

"Donna Reed," she replied. "People tell me I do favor her a bit, but I can't see it."

"No," said Verity. "I can't either."

Chapter 10

Unlike Big Al Radwanski, Wilder and Verity didn't make it to church. They were in no hurry to exit the Murphy bed.

"I had a good time at the dance last night, Wildest."

"Yeah, me too."

"Did you like Ruth Edna?"

"Sure, she seemed nice."

"She has quite the pair, don't you think?"

"Does she? I didn't notice."

"God, I've got you so well trained."

"Did you really think Ginger Rogers was married to Roy?"

"Of course not. What do you take me for? I was just being a good conversationalist. And Ruth Edna looks like Donna Reed like I look like Greta Garbo–although I do have Garbo's slim figure. I think ol' Tom may be making some inquiries about you."

"Why do you say that?"

"Because when we were dancing, he asked me in what jurisdiction the vandalism incident took place."

"He probably thinks I jumped bail. What did you tell him?"

"Being no fool, I said Parkersburg. That reminds me, I had another epiphany."

"What this time?"

"That note that Dot left for her parents. It may have been intended to deceive."

"How so?"

"She said Boyd's route was mostly through Ohio. That now seems in doubt. It could have been a lie to throw everyone off her trail."

"I don't think Dot's the kind of girl to lie. And I've been calling fairs in western Pennsylvania too. He's not showing up there either."

"There's a whole state west of here, honey. Called Indiana. What if he's hawking his green slime in Indiana?"

"I never thought of that."

"Where did you get that list of fairs?"

"From the library in Erie. There's a directory of fairs and festivals. Put out by a magazine called *Amusement Business*."

"We could see if they have it at the library here. Maybe phone a few fairs in the Hoosier state."

"Good idea. But I expect the library's closed on Sunday."

"We'll go there first thing tomorrow."

"What should we do today?"

"We'll take a swim in the lake. Then I'll make brunch. That's breakfast for people who rise fashionably late. Then we'll fool around in bed some more. Then we'll go into town and have dinner at a nice restaurant. My treat since you got stuck buying most of the beer last night. How does that sound?"

"Sounds like a plan. But you don't have to pay. Are you ready to get out of bed?"

"What's the rush, Wild Guy? Are you tired of me already?"

He wasn't, although he was surprised at the unflagging enthusiasm she brought to the task.

The elegant restaurant Verity had seen in the hotel downtown was closed on Sunday nights. They had to scramble for an alternative. It appeared that many Mt. Vernon restaurateurs preferred to spend this night at home with their families. A possible extra incentive to close was Ohio's blue laws, which banned the sale of alcohol on Sunday.

They drove around town and wound up in the coffee shop of a bowling alley. It was league night for church groups, who didn't mind bowling cold sober. Wilder ordered the deluxe turkey and bacon club sandwich. It was constructed with *four* slices of toast and was the tallest club sandwich he had ever seen. Six toothpicks held the monstrosity together, three piercing each half through the many layers. Verity had the 21 Shrimps in a Basket. She kept track as she ate and counted only 19.

"Your basket did appear full," Wilder pointed out. "You may have received slightly larger shrimp, hence the reduced amount."

"Then the menu should list it as an *average* of 21 shrimps. Or they could say *up to* 21 shrimps. Or a *surprise* number of shrimps. But no, they were very specific. By doing so, they leave their shrimp patrons feeling cheated."

"Are you still hungry? Did that meal not fill you up?"

"I'm quite full. That is not the issue here. The issue is whether it is right to lie to your customers."

The waitress brought over two slices of lemon meringue pie.

"Uh, ma'am, we didn't order these," said Wilder.

"No charge, hon. We're not supposed to have any pie left over when we close on Sunday. So after six o'clock we give 'em away. Enjoy!"

"There you have it," said Wilder when she walked away.

"There I have what?" asked Verity.

"Not only did your shrimps in a basket provide a satisfying meal, but now you're receiving a free dessert."

"Oh, now I see, Wildest. You're one of those people without principles. Who can be bought off with free pie."

"I can be bought off with good free pie. And this is excellent."

"It is rather nice. It goes well with the din of crashing bowling pins and your sophistry."

"I suppose you expected to receive *21 pieces* of free pie."

"I do feel that is the least they owe me for violating my trust. Are we going bowling next? I should warn you I've never tried bowling."

"Some other time, Varsity. All the alleys are reserved tonight."

"Wow. Who knew bowling was reserved for the elite? How much do those boys make who set up the pins? It looks like an exciting job."

"Not much. The alley where I bowled back home only paid 35 cents an hour."

"So little? That's medieval!"

"They do make a little extra in tips. And if business is slow, some places let the pin boys bowl for free."

"It's indoor work, Wild Bug, so I guess it's out as a career for you. Are there wild throws in bowling? Do people get knocked out by flying bowling balls?"

"I've never heard of that happening. Pin boys do get beaned by ricocheting pins sometimes. You have to stay alert back there. And Amy, Dot's friend, once got her finger stuck in a ball and got dragged halfway down an alley. They had to put it in a splint."

After a mild tug of war over the check they decided to go dutch. They watched the bowlers for a few minutes, then drove back to the cabin to give the Murphy bed another workout.

The Mt. Vernon library opened at nine o'clock. They had a copy of the fair directory, but it was shelved in the reference section and couldn't be checked out. The reference librarian kept a sharp eye on them, so pilferage was not possible. Wilder copied the relevant data into his notebook while Verity leafed through *Time* magazine. Crime-fighter J. Edgar Hoover gazed out menacingly from the cover.

"*Time's* critic likes the new Burt Lancaster movie," she noted. "If Robert Mitchum doesn't start showing more interest, I may throw him over for Burt."

"Was he born in Ohio?" asked Wilder, still copying.

"Hardly. Burt is one of the innumerable talented people born in Manhattan. His real name is Burton. Where do parents get these names? Can you imagine naming your tiny little son Burton? Of course, it's still miles ahead of Wilder."

Wilder didn't have much hope, but the third Indiana fair he tried with the sick twin's transfusion plea came up a winner.

"I'll send someone right over to the exhibition hall," said the gal, sounding concerned.

"Don't bother," said Wilder. "I was only kidding. This is the fair in Richmond, right?"

"It sure is," she replied. "And we don't appreciate crank calls!"

She hung up. Wilder did the same and turned to Verity, loitering outside the booth.

"He's at the Wayne County Fair in Richmond, Indiana."

"God, I am so smart. And your girlfriend is a big fat liar."

They hurried back to the car to consult the map. Richmond was just across the border on U.S. 40.

"We take 36 into Columbus and head west from there," said Wilder. "We should get there around dinner time."

"How nice. You can take Dot out for a big thick steak–assuming you can pry her away from her man."

"We'll cross that bridge when we come to it. I just want to talk to her. Let's go back to the cabin and pack."

"Do we have time for a quick one?"

"Sorry. We have to make tracks. We have a lot of miles to cover today."

"OK, but just keep in mind that your sex life may be cratering in a few hours. And I don't think those Army posts are coed."

They packed hurriedly and returned the cabin key to Mr. Murchfoble. He put down his newspaper and said, "I hope you've patched up your differences."

"We haven't been fighting," said Wilder. "We get along fine."

"What was that yelling I kept hearing from your cabin?" he asked.

Verity blushed. "I, uh, like to sing when I do the dishes."

"Well, you must be one neat housekeeper, 'cause you were washing those plates all hours of the day and night. I can't say I hope you come back 'cause to be honest the missus won't rent to you again. She comes from very upright folks. I barely make the grade myself most of the time."

"Damn, Wild Dog," said Verity as they were driving away. "We just got tossed out of our love nest. Was I making that much noise?"

"That cabin had single-layer walls, Varsity. No sound-proofing. You did hit some high notes once in a while."

"I can barely get a grunt or two out of you. Was I having that much better of a time?"

"I guess guys put most of our force into expelling the wad."

"That's the grossest thing anyone's ever said to me."

"Sorry to be so graphic. I just don't think you'll find many guys who are screamers."

"I am not a screamer. I just vociferate energetically at times."

"Right. Keep your eyes peeled for the turnoff for Route 36."

In New Rome, just west of Columbus, they were pulled over by a motorcycle cop and cited for having a dusty taillight and crooked license plate.

"What are you doing so far from home in this rat trap?" he asked, handing Wilder back his license.

"We're going to visit my brother in Indiana," lied Wilder.

"Crossing state lines, huh? What is your relationship to this underage female?"

"She's my wife. And she's 18, just like me. Show the man your ring, darling."

Verity extended her left arm to show off her budget sparkler. "I hope this won't take long, officer. I can feel the baby kicking up a storm."

The cop eyed her midriff dubiously, then tore the ticket off his pad. "You can pay this at City Hall, or you can pay me cash only. The fine is $10."

Wilder took out his thin wallet and handed over two fives. The cop pocketed the bills.

"Why does it matter that my license plate is crooked?" asked Wilder.

"I need to be able to read a plate from the back of a motorcycle at sixty miles an hour. The digits must be absolutely clear and level."

"But I was barely going thirty."

"You could have rocketed through here doing ninety. I'm not going to risk my neck trying to chase you down. I need to read the plate."

"My car can't go ninety."

"Immaterial. The law's the law. Be glad I'm not hauling you in to subject this crate to a complete mechanical inspection."

The cop stowed away his pad and roared off on his three-wheeled Harley.

"I bet you just bought that guy a fancy lunch," said Verity.

"You'd think we were in Russia or something," said Wilder, starting the car. "They don't teach you about crooked graft like that in civics class."

"I do like a man on a motorcycle though. He looked a bit like Buster Crabbe. I sensed he was undressing me with his eyes."

"More likely he was undressing my wallet."

"You should wear sexy breeches like his that flare out above your boots."

"I don't have any damn boots."

"Do cops call them jodhpurs I wonder? I bet they have their own virile police jargon term. In any case they wouldn't work without boots. They'd look perfectly silly with your juvenile low-tops."

They stopped in Springfield for a late lunch at the Cave Diner. The waitress in the pink hard hat remembered them.

"How was your camping trip?" she asked, handing them menus. "Did you get hit by all that rain last week?"

"Our tent got soaked," said Verity. "We had to sleep in the car stacked on top of each other."

"Well, that could be fun too," she chuckled.

Still reeling from his fine, Wilder limited himself to a 25-cent bowl of chili (called Lava Chili on the menu). He asked the waitress if she'd heard any complaints about New Rome.

"Worst speed trap in the state, hon. I guess they nailed you, huh? What were you doing, 36 in a 35 mile-an-hour zone?"

"No, dusty taillight," said Verity.

"Right. You need to go slow and drive a very clean car in that town. They got more cops than residents. I always detour around it. I suggest you do the same."

When you cross the border on U.S. 40 into Indiana, the terrain remains just as flat. The flora doesn't change. The farms, houses, and stores look about the same as they did in Ohio. The license plates sport a different color scheme, and many more businesses feature the word "Hoosier" in their names. A sign at the Richmond city limits identified it as the birthplace of Wendell Stanley, Winner of the Nobel Prize.

"You ever heard of that guy?" asked Wilder.

"Sure. His plays are performed all over the world."

"Really?"

"Just kidding, Wildness. I have no idea who he is."

"I bet if they had any movie stars born here, they'd be bumping that dude off the sign."

"This state is a complete blank to me, Wild One. It has never in my life come up in conversation until I met you. Illinois has Chicago, Abe Lincoln, and assorted gangsters, but what does this state have? Besides your girlfriend, I mean."

"It has the Indianapolis 500. They run it on Memorial Day. They have some steel mills up around Gary. The Ku Klux Klan used to be big here back in the 1920s."

"Gee, that fills in some blanks."

"Booth Tarkington's from Indiana. We read his Penrod book in the seventh grade. And Cole Porter's from Peru, Indiana."

"Cole Porter, huh? I suppose he does make up a bit for the KKK. I didn't realize he was Peruvian."

Monday was a slow day at the fair. They parked in a half-empty lot at the fairgrounds.

"Why don't you stay here?" said Wilder. "This shouldn't take long."

"Dream on, buddy. I wouldn't miss meeting your missing Miss Dot for all the world."

"Well, try to behave yourself. And take off that damn fake wedding ring."

"Are you kidding? If she's shacking with that stud, I'm the biggest revenge you've got. Just put your arm around me and tell her what a swell time you had on our honeymoon."

It was not difficult to spot the Miracle Creme concession. So many green cans were stacked up in the booth it glowed in the distance like Oz's Emerald City. A man who resembled Cary Grant's more handsome brother had a big chrome microphone slung on a cord around his neck and was trying to attract a crowd.

"You've heard about it, friends. Your neighbors swear by it. Your children clamor for it. Those green men in the flying saucers are invading our skies looking for it. No, you can't buy it in stores. Now's your chance to discover the real, authentic Miracle Creme. Here comes a handsome couple. Step right up folks. Don't be shy. Tell me, miss, would you like more body in your hair?"

"Actually I'd like more body in my body," replied Verity, flirting shamelessly.

"We're looking for Dolores Bateson," said Wilder. "Where is she? What have you done with her?"

Boyd switched off his microphone. "Dolores Bateson, huh? I do know her. What do you want with her?"

"I'm a friend of hers from Erie. Nobody's heard from her in weeks!"

"Now, hold on there, Tarzan. I didn't realize our Dot was so behind in her correspondence. She's fine."

"Where is she? I'm not going to ask you again!"

"I don't really care for your tone, sonny. Dolores is not here. She works at our production facility in Akron."

"What? She's not traveling with you?"

"I believe I just made that clear. She's a production

worker at our plant. A hard worker and easy on the eyes. What's not to like? She brought me her report card back in Erie. She got straight As in chemistry so I hired her."

"You don't make this stuff in your trailer?"

"I sell hundreds of cases a week, lad. I'd need a trailer the size of the Hindenburg to keep up with demand."

"Where in Akron is she? What's the address?"

"I don't give that out as a rule. There are companies big and small finagling to nab my formula. I'm surrounded by spies. Hell, I'm a bigger target than Coca-Cola. All they offer is sugar water with bubbles. My product can change your life."

"I want that address!" Wilder insisted.

"Hey, keep your shirt on. Here's my card. It's got the factory phone number on it. You can call Dolores and arrange to meet her off-site–assuming she wants to talk to some belligerent youth with no manners."

"He's been going steady with her for 14 years," Verity explained. "She left town without a word."

"That usually indicates the romance has been terminated," said Boyd. "When women make up their minds, you can get whiplash from the jolt. I'm speaking here from experience. And what's your interest in this affair, miss?"

"I'm the replacement girlfriend. I've been easing him down off the cliff."

"Well, from the looks of him, I'd say he still has a ways to go."

"We met your competitor, the Magic Creem man," said Wilder. "He told me to tell you he hopes you die of a massive stroke."

"Jerry's a real card. He's my cousin, you know. He used to work for me. He managed to steal part of my formula, but hasn't got it quite right. He tried his version on his scalp. That's why he has to wear that silly rug."

"You have marvelous hair," said Verity.

"I'm sure you'd enjoy running your fingers through it, miss. That can be arranged. You want to ditch this boy scout and have dinner with me later? I know a good steak house in town that's open late."

"I'd love to, Boyd, but I'm on my way to Frisco."

"Well, here's a can of the real thing to remember me by. Rub a little on your intimate areas and think about me. If you're not tingling all over, give me a call and I'll see what I can do to improve matters."

"I may do that. Thanks, Boyd. And what's up with your cousin's ears?"

"Hard delivery. He about killed my aunt being hatched. Even back then the guy had a swelled head. He came out feet first and his big head got stuck. The doc had to get aggressive with the forceps. Things went snap, crackle, and pop. Left him with ears that scare off the chicks."

"I'm glad that didn't happen to you," she said.

"Yeah, sweetheart, me too. My offer's still open. Come back anytime. Hang out in the booth and help me move some stock."

"I'll bet you've moved quite a lot of stock."

"I rarely get complaints in that department," he replied with a wink.

Wilder didn't speak until they got back to the car.

"You didn't have to swoon so much over that guy."

"Actually, I thought I was rather restrained. I'd heard about bedroom eyes. They were always a topic of conversation back at my high school. And now I've seen the real thing. But aren't you thrilled, Wild Bee? Your virginal girlfriend's sullied reputation has been restored. She's not buffing the pickle, she's stirring industrial vats of Miracle Creme in Akron."

"I never really thought she was making it with that Boyd guy."

"Hah! Don't give me that. You suspected the worst. That's why you were so miserable."

"If we leave now, we might be able to make it to Akron by midnight."

"Count me out for that trip, Wildness. You can drop me off at U.S. 40 on your way out of town."

"What! You're not coming with me?"

"No. That's not the direction I'm headed. You go have your reunion with Dot and live happily ever after. Think of me when you're shoveling snow in Erie. I'm on my way west to sunny California."

"Is this another test, Varsity? Should I wail and plead?"

"It's not a test, lover. It's sayonara. It's the parting of the ways. It's been fun, but all good things must come to an end. There, I've run out of cliches, so let's get going."

He drove back through town and pulled over to the curb on Highway 40.

"Why don't I take you to the bus station, Varsity? You can catch a Greyhound back to New York. Then in September you can take the train to California. Or even fly there."

"Not on the program, Wild Thing. I'm hitching across the country. I'm sticking out my thumb and heading west. So drag my duffel out of your missing back seat, and kiss me good-bye. I need to catch a lift before it gets dark."

Wilder tore a sheet of paper from his notebook and wrote down his address and phone number.

"Write to me, Varsity. Send me your address and phone number. Call me if anything goes wrong."

"Will do, Wild Zone."

They got out of the car and had a long clinch in front of the Happy Hoosier Baby Emporium.

"I'll miss you, Varsity."

"Probably not that much, but thanks for the sentiments. Don't forget: if you enlist in the Marines, I'll never speak to you again."

"I'll keep that in mind."

"So hit the road, Wildness. Try not to get lost or killed in your Death Car. Tell ol' Dot I said she should be nicer to you. She should be grateful to have you."

"OK. And you take care. Watch what cars you get into."

"Too late, love. I already got into yours."

Verity shouldered her duffel and walked away. She didn't look back.

Chapter 11

Wilder spent the night in his car in the empty lot of a funeral parlor in south Akron. Looming in the distance was the largest factory he'd ever seen. Its thousands of windows were ablaze with light as the graveyard shift toiled away making tires. A string of red lights flashed on and off at the summit of its tall brick chimney. He assumed it was the source of the sulphur smell that pervaded the neighborhood. He didn't get much sleep. Too much driving. When he closed his eyes, an endless highway rolled past on the inside of his eyelids.

No one answered the phone at the Miracle Creme plant until 8:01. The girl said "Hold on" and went to find his requested party.

"Hello," said Dolores, sounding wary.

'It's me. Wilder."

"How did you get this number?"

"From your boss Boyd in Richmond."

"You went to Indiana, Wilder?"

"I went all over. I'm wondering what happened to you."

"I can't take personal calls, Wilder. Not while I'm working. Where are you?"

"Where else? I'm in Akron. I got in late last night."

"Well, you should go home. Aren't you supposed to be at welding school?"

"I'm not going anywhere until I see you. When do you get off work?"

"Not till late. This is our busy season. I take my lunch at 12:30. I guess we could meet at a restaurant close by."

"I'll be there. Where is it?"

"It's a cafeteria across the street from the Goodyear plant on East Market Street. I forget the exact address."

"I'll find it. I'll see you then."

"OK. You shouldn't have come all this way, Wilder."

"We'll talk about it at lunch."

Wilder located East Market Street on his map. It was one of the city's main commercial streets and would be easy to find. He drove to downtown Akron, parked, and walked around to kill time. It was a big downtown with busy stores, many movie theaters, and several large department stores. A block west of Main Street was a bustling Negro district. Nearby was a block-long brick hotel that housed a tavern called the Rubber Room. According to a sign in the lobby, all of the bar furnishings were made from rubber. Wilder imagined its inebriated patrons lurching about and bouncing off the rubber walls. He passed a florist's shop and thought of buying flowers, but decided that was a bad idea. Instead he went into W.T. Grant's and bought a shower cap on sale. He figured she could always use that.

The hours crawled by, but eventually he found himself in front of the cafeteria at 12:29. He almost didn't recognize her. She was wearing a blue factory smock and had cut her hair nearly as short as his. No make-up, not even lipstick. She gave him a brief hug, but didn't kiss him.

"I like your sunglasses," she said. "You look like Gregory Peck in that war movie."

"Thanks. So what's with the boys' regular haircut?"

"It's stifling where I work. I couldn't stand all that hair in the heat. You need a haircut."

"Yeah, well I've had other things on my mind."

The cafeteria was a busy place geared for factory workers; the servings were generous and the prices modest. They got trays and went down the line. Dot got the daily special, which on this day was salt pork with lima beans. It came with a little dish of coleslaw and another of custard. Plus a dinner roll and tab of butter. Plus coffee or tea. All for 45 cents. Wilder got the ham plate special, which was 65 cents. Wilder picked up the tab. They found a table for two in the back.

"What's in the sack?" she asked, sipping her ice tea.

"I picked you up a shower cap."

"Thanks. I could have used it when I had long hair. How's your ham?"

"Good. It's not too salty."

He told her about his recent discovery of Siamese pie.

"I do like a good pot pie. But you have to be careful, Wilder. All that pie dough can pack on the pounds. I eat here every day. I always have the special, since it's such a good deal."

"You're aiming to eat all those lima beans?"

It was the largest pile of lima beans he had ever seen, dwarfing the few pieces of pork.

"I don't mind them. Yesterday was beans and franks. I doubt they could feature a pot pie at these prices."

"So, Dot, you want to tell me what's going on?"

"I thought you were going away, Wilder. For two months. That was your plan. I thought the separation was a good idea. You know, to think about things. Then you up and decided you didn't like welding school. If you were coming back, then I had to leave. So I did. Amy found me this job."

"So she did know where you were. She claimed she didn't."

"I told her not to tell anyone. Were you the sneak behind that phone call about the bogus scholarship?"

"Amy told you about that, huh?"

"As if some school I didn't even apply to was handing me a scholarship. Who was that girl who called?"

"Just someone I met on the road. I'm still not getting why you had to leave, Dot. Did I do something wrong?"

"It's not you, Wilder. It's me. We're not in high school any more. This is the real world. We have to think about things like adults. You have no direction, Wilder. That's OK. You're young. Why should you? You're going in the Army, and who knows what you'll do after that? I sure don't. The last thing you need is me hanging around your neck."

"So why didn't we just talk about this?"

"I told you. I had to get away to think. Get away from my parents. And get away from you. I'm sorry you came looking for me. I guess I didn't think you would. What are you driving anyway?"

"That old Plymouth that belonged to my uncle."

"Your parents let you leave in that heap?"

"I left them a note."

"Your dad didn't report it stolen?"

"I guess not. He gave me a break for once in my life. So that's it? You're dumping me?"

"What choice do I have, Wilder? I'm supposed to wait for you all those years while you're in the Army? Then what happens? You come back to Erie and get some factory job you hate? We live in some dumpy little apartment somewhere? Face it, Wilder, what do you have to offer a girl?"

"I don't know. I thought we were pretty close."

"We were, Wilder. We are. But you can't live on hopes and dreams. I'm saving up to go to nursing school. I know where I'm going."

"Are you seeing someone here in Akron?"

"Oh, sure. I work six days a week in a sweatbox factory. On Sunday I try to cool off a little and do my laundry. I have a real lively social life."

"You live around here?"

"I rent a room in a house a few blocks away. It's not very nice, but it's cheap. I can save money. And it's close to work so I don't need a car."

"You could have written me a letter. And said all that."

"I tried to. I started a letter to you almost every night. I couldn't find the words. It's been really hard. Some nights I barely sleep. I don't want to hurt you, Wilder, but we have to face reality. It can't work out with us."

"So you never want to see me again?"

"Who knows, Wilder? Who knows where we'll be someday? In five years maybe we'll both be in a better place. Maybe it will work out then. But I wouldn't count on it. People change. They grow apart. Life goes on. You'll find some nice girl and get married. You'll forget all about me."

"I'm sure I won't do that. At least not the last part."

"Are you going back to welding school?"

"I can't. My dad's taken my place."

"Really?"

"Yeah, he's learning to weld instead of me. More power to him."

"I like your mom, Wilder, but I never much cared for your dad. Don't tell him I said that."

"He's OK most of the time. He gets under my skin sometimes. You know your dad's here in Ohio. He's looking for you too."

"More good news! Why can't people just leave me alone! Did you tell him where I am?"

"I haven't talked to him. You're getting kind of antisocial in your old age, Dot."

"I just have less patience for people trying to run my life. Please don't tell my parents where I am."

"OK, sure. If you don't want me to. Can I tell them you're OK?"

"Better not. I know they'll pry it all out of you if they think you know something. I've got to go. I can't be late getting back. I need this job."

"So what's in Miracle Creme? What's the secret formula?"

"Don't ask me. The stuff we make it from isn't labeled. Most of it comes in big drums. Only Boyd knows the actual ingredients. He handles all the buying of supplies personally. We just measure and mix and cook and pour. I think the green is from some commercial dye. Don't ask me why he chose that color."

Wilder left a quarter on the table as a tip and they left.

"Can I walk you back to your job?"

"Sorry. They'd fire me if they thought I showed anyone where I work. It's almost as secret as if we're making A-bombs."

They embraced and she kissed him.

"You take it easy, Wilder. Don't get yourself shot in the Army."

"I'll try not to. You want to give me your mailing address?"

"I better not. My dad might weasel it out of you."

"Will I see you at Christmas time?"

"I don't know. Maybe. I can't make any promises. Bye, dear. Please don't follow me. You'll get me in trouble."

"I won't. I'm leaving. I'll see you around sometime."

"Maybe. And thanks for the shower cap."

"My pleasure."

Wilder didn't follow her. He walked back to his car and looked at the map. If he went north on Route 44 and then east on Highway 20, he might make it back to Erie by dinner time. He wondered what his mother would be cooking. With his father out on strike and no money coming in it might be something simple like potato soup. Or something fresh from her garden. When he was a little kid during the Depression, his father trapped rabbits for the table. He always had his job, but sometimes the screen-door plant only operated one day a week if that. He would skin his catch in the field and pass it off as possum so as not to make Wilder cry by killing a bunny. The rabbit traps were still hanging on the wall of the garage.

Wilder stopped for gas on North Main Street. A filling station occupied each corner of the intersection, and they were having a gas war. Wilder filled up his tank for 19 cents a gallon. He got his windshield washed, his oil checked, and was offered his choice of a pressed-glass candy dish or a Hollywood key chain featuring a full-color portrait of a movie star on a metal disc.

"I'll take the key chain," said Wilder.

"All we have left is Andy Devine or Gabby Hayes," said the attendant.

"That's OK. I'll take Gabby."

The sun was in his eyes as he pulled out of the station, and he nearly ran over a woman pushing a baby carriage.

"Watch it, buddy," she said.

A tiny hand rose up out of the carriage and flashed him the finger.

Chapter 12

Parking in downtown Indianapolis on a busy Wednesday morning was nearly impossible. Risking a ticket, Wilder parked in a loading zone on Pennsylvania Avenue across from a landscaped square housing the Indiana War Memorial. He found the address he was looking for and entered the building.

"Can I help you?" asked the receptionist.

"Do you rent out rooms?"

"Not to men. This is the YWCA."

"Can you tell me if you have a girl named Verity Warren staying here?"

The receptionist checked her guest book. "Sorry. We have no one by that name registered."

"Are there other YWCAs in this town?"

"We have another location for colored girls. Is she by any chance a Negro?"

"Uh, no. She's not. Well, thanks anyway."

Hurrying back to his car, Wilder was surprised to see Verity sitting on his fender. She was eating a donut and sipping from a paper cup.

"You know, Wild Beast, you're parked here illegally."

Being careful not to spill her coffee, he embraced and kissed her.

"I thought I would never find you, Varsity. This has got to be a miracle!"

"Well, if there had been one more person in front of me

at the donut shop, we likely would have missed each other entirely. It must be fate."

"Where were you?"

"The Y was full up, so I spent the night around the corner in this town's version of a flophouse. Pricier than the Y and all the bugs you could swat. I registered under the name Ann Page in case my father has detectives on my trail. May I ask what you're doing here?"

"Looking for you mostly. Want to hit the road together?"

"Could be. Where are you headed?"

"I thought I'd check out Berkeley. That's a college town in California."

"What about your menacing draft board?"

"I expect they'll find me if they really want me."

"What about your doting parents?"

"They'll get by. They were going to lose me to the Army anyway. We should get going before I get a ticket or get towed."

"Right. Well, toss in my duffel and let's ride."

Wilder proceeded slowly through heavy city traffic.

"How was Akron, honey? Did you connect to your missing Dot?"

"I did. She cut me loose. She said I lacked direction and didn't have anything to offer a girl."

"She's more perceptive than I gave her credit for."

"Jesus, Varsity, am I that useless?"

"Not to me, Wildest. People who have their lives totally figured out at our age are deficient in one vital quality."

"What's that?"

"Imagination."

"I don't know. You may be right. Dot did say there was a possibility we could get back together in a few years when we're more settled."

"Don't count on it, old sport. The only thing in the world more useless to a girl than an old boyfriend is an ex-husband. Did she mention another beau?"

"I asked her. She said all she does is work in the factory and do her laundry on Sunday."

"That's a lie, of course."

"Really? You think so?"

"There's always someone else in the picture when you get dumped, Wildness. That is the one immutable law of romance."

"Damn, I wish she'd told me."

"She was sparing your feelings. I give her credit for that. There's a reason I was so much easier to track down than that slippery chick."

"Why was that?"

"Because I wanted to be found. Destiny desires us to cleave. You think this bucket of bolts can make it to California?"

"It's been sounding better. I think all that driving has freed up its valves or burned off the carbon or something. The engine is running smoother and my gas mileage has improved. And you left behind your can of Miracle Creme. I had some time to kill in Akron so I smeared some on my ball joints and tie rods. Now there's less play in the steering and the car tracks straighter."

"Another triumph for darling Boyd. Even the mouse aromas may be dissipating at last."

"I hope you don't mind me asking, Varsity. How are you fixed for gas money?"

"Not bad. I still have over $800 in my duffel."

"Where'd you get all that money? Did you roll some rich guy?"

"Graduation gifts. Naturally, I requested cash. They never suspected I'd use their largesse to fund my escape. What gifts did you receive?"

"A fountain pen with my name engraved on it."

"That can come in handy if you have amnesia and forget your identity."

"And I guess my dead uncle gave me this car."

"A generous gesture on his part. Wait! Stop right here!"

"Wha– what's wrong?"

"I need to visit that store. We need some music. I have no idea what's topping the Hit Parade this week."

Wilder pulled in and parked beside the store. Verity removed the fake wedding ring from her purse and slipped it on her finger.

"You kept that, huh?" said Wilder.

"I should say so, darling. It's the only thing you've ever given me."

"That's not true. What about your nice hat?"

"Oh, right, Diamond Jim. Correction: it's the most expensive thing you've ever given me."

"That reminds me, sweetheart, I've got something for you."

Wilder removed a small object from his pocket and handed it to her.

"How curious. A key chain bearing the likeness of a bearded fellow, possibly Sigmund Freud. Truly a gift from your deepest subconscious."

"It's not Sigmund Freud, Varsity. It's Gabby Hayes, the cowboy movie star."

"Ah, even kinkier than I had supposed. I'll treasure it always."

The radio store featured all the top brands and displayed a large selection of portable models. Verity zeroed in on a Magnavox. About the size of the Manhattan phone directory it had a leatherette exterior with built-in handle and extendable antenna.

"This is the tiniest radio I've ever seen!" she exclaimed.

"You won't ever find one smaller," said the salesman. "They've shrunk those tubes as small as they can go. It features the latest superheterodyne circuitry with two bands: AM and FM. You don't get so much static from your FM stations. The fidelity is remarkable."

"And are there many FM stations?" she asked.

"Not many as of yet, but more are on the way. You'll be prepared for 1950 and beyond with this radio."

"How many batteries does it take?" asked Wilder.

"It uses eight D cells, sir. But don't worry. A full set is included in the price. Only $69.95 plus tax. It has a large six-inch speaker with dual cones for enhanced tone. Personally, I think the sound is superior to some of our expensive table models."

Verity had another question, "Is there an adapter cord to power it from our car's cigarette lighter?"

"Sorry, I've never heard of one. That's not a bad idea though. You'd think somebody would make one."

"What do you think, dear? My husband's a subscriber to *Popular Mechanics*. He's fully informed on the latest electronics wizardry."

"It's your money, Varsity. I think it's a reputable brand. You can buy it if you want to. But it's going to eat batteries. How long does a set last?"

"That depends on your location," said the salesman. "Of course, in fringe areas it's going to use more power to pull in those distant stations."

"I think I'll take it," said Verity. "We can get critical weather updates to dodge those killer tornadoes in Oklahoma."

While Verity completed the transaction, Wilder wandered over to the television display. All the TVs were tuned to a program featuring a woman demonstrating how to iron socks on a Model 88 Ironrite mangle iron.

"Can I help you? asked the TV salesman, who was older

and more distinguished-looking than the radio salesman.

"Just looking, thanks. That sure is a massive TV screen."

"It's RCA's latest model. A full nine inches in diameter. Viewers say it's just like having their own private movie theater."

"We're heading cross country by car. We're not in the market for a TV yet."

"Confidentially, it might be good to wait. Sylvania's supposed to be coming out with a model with an eleven-inch screen by Christmas."

"Wow, that would be impressive."

Verity kissed him on the way out of the store.

"What was that for?" he asked.

"For stopping here and indulging my whims. We're going to have fun, Wild Man. We're going to see the purple mountains' majesty and the fruited plains."

"What are the fruited plains anyway?"

"I really can't say. But I expect we'll be encountering giant billboards advertising their particulars."

"You want to stick to U.S. 40, Varsity? It's a straight shot west, but it's got a lot of truck traffic."

"I don't know, Wildest. I'm in no hurry. Do you want to wander a bit?"

"Sure. Let's wander."

They returned to the car and Verity switched on her radio. Perry Como was singing the week's Number One hit, "Some Enchanted Evening."

"Ugh, Perry Como," said Verity, turning the dial. "How can a guy who's Italian sound that desperately white?"

"Well, he is white," said Wilder.

"That's no excuse."

She tuned across the band and found Nat King Cole singing "Exactly Like You."

She sang along to the radio:

I know why I've waited

Know why I've been blue

I prayed each night for someone

Exactly like you . . .

"Exactly like me?" Wilder inquired, glancing over with a smile.

"Not exactly like you, Wild Hunk. More like Robert Mitchum. But you'll do."

Verity switched off her radio to conserve the batteries and studied her map.

"You want to go through Chicago?" she asked.

"I don't know, Varsity. Those big cities really know how to ding your wallet. I once had to pay 50 cents an hour just to park in Cleveland."

"Sorry, city of broad shoulders and tourist gouging, we'll see you some other time. Besides, I doubt Chicago offers anything that wasn't done earlier and better in New York."

"How about this, Varsity? DOT DITCHED A GUY. FOR ANOTHER ON THE SLY. NOW WE RIDE WEST. IT'S ALL FOR THE BEST. BURMA-SHAVE."

"Not bad, Wild Poet. Are you over that girl at last?"

"I'm working on it."

Henry the Recycler

HENRY'S FATHER was eating breakfast and reading the newspaper. It was a widely known fact that he was incapable of eating breakfast without a newspaper at hand.

Henry arrived at the table dressed as he usually did: in striped T-shirt and cargo pants.

Henry was nearly 11 years old, but looked younger. This annoyed him, a fact which he had noted on a list he kept titled "Henry Oldham's Annoyances."

Henry loved cargo pants. He appreciated all the roomy pockets. His were an extra-special kind: on hot days you could unzip the bottom parts and turn the pants into shorts. Henry expected that he would wear this exact style of pants for the rest of his life. He doubted he would ever get married, but should such an event occur, he expected to arrive for the ceremony dressed in zip-off cargo pants. If his bride objected, the wedding would have to be cancelled.

Henry greeted his parents and poured his usual bowl of cornflakes. No one suspected that this was a day that Henry would never forget.

Henry's little sister Sally sat in her highchair and refused to eat her oatmeal.

She had come about in a rather interesting way. Several years before, Henry's father had gone out one Saturday morning and not returned for hours. He missed lunch and didn't phone.

"That's odd," said Henry's mother, looking concerned.

"He told me he was just going down to the hardware store."

Finally, late in the afternoon, he returned–followed by a tow truck pulling an dusty old car.

"What the heck is that?" asked Henry's mother (not quoting exactly).

"Isn't it great?" said Henry's dad. "It's the same make and model as my very first car!"

"Does it run?" asked Henry's mom, looking dubious.

"It will when I finish restoring it," he replied.

Henry helped his dad push the grimy old hulk into their single-car garage. Henry noticed that the interior of the car looked just as bad as the outside.

"If you can drag that heap home," said Henry's mother in her severest voice, "then I can have another baby."

Henry didn't see how cars and babies were connected, but a few months later his mother announced that she was expecting Henry's little sister.

Henry feared that a baby would be annoying, but he found that Sally was rather interesting and sometimes did amusing things. His father often exclaimed, "Babies are better than TV!"

Henry wouldn't have gone that far, but he generally regarded his sister with bemused tolerance. Lately, her favorite word was "no." For example, you could ask her if she wanted to go to the mall and get some great new toys.

"No!" Sally would reply. Then her face would crinkle up and she would start to cry.

Henry's mother, who read a lot of books about babies, said Sally was now at the "defiance stage." She didn't get annoyed when Sally said "no," but Henry knew it would be a different story if he tried it.

Henry munched his cornflakes and read the comics page. The year before, his doctor had discovered that Henry was gluten-intolerant. This meant he couldn't eat foods made with wheat–including such appetizing things as normal cakes, cookies, pizzas, and pasta. Now, when the family went out to eat, Henry's mother brought along a special bun to give to the cook for Henry's burger. Henry found this annoying, but he didn't complain. He knew there was no point complaining about something that couldn't be changed.

"Here's an interesting ad," said Henry's dad, looking up from his newspaper. "This could be for you, Hank."

"What is it," asked Henry.

"It's under Jobs Offered. The ad says: Recyclers wanted. Students welcome. Then there's a phone number and an address."

"It could be a scam," said Henry's mother, struggling to spoon some oatmeal into her defiant daughter.

"How could that be a scam?" asked Henry's dad.

"Oh, I don't know, Dave," she replied. "They could make you buy some over-priced plastic bags, then send you out to scavenge for cans."

"I think I'll check into it," said Henry, a great believer in recycling. He also enjoyed earning and saving money.

Before he left for school, Henry looked up the address on his father's computer. It was around the block from the Main Library. Since Henry lived in a neighborhood of modest older houses just north of downtown, he was permitted to walk the few blocks to the library on his own.

When he returned from school for lunch, Henry called the number. He made an appointment with the man who answered to drop by that afternoon after school. His mother was wary, but gave her permission. She told him that if they tried to sell him anything, he should leave immediately. And if they gave him any trouble, he should call her or 9-1-1 on his cell phone.

"OK, Mom," he agreed.

"And don't let them offer you any wheat snacks."

"I know, Mom," he said. "I never eat anything with gluten in it."

Henry may have looked younger than his age, but he exhibited the maturity of a much older person. This was a comfort to his mother, who was inclined to worry.

At school they did some long division and discussed volcanoes. Henry enjoyed science class, but wished they could discuss something besides volcanoes and dinosaurs.

He was Henry to his teacher, but his friends called him Hank. At times, they altered his name to suit the circumstances. For example, when they went swimming, they called him "Sank" (even though he was a good swimmer). On those rare occasions when Henry got in trouble with a teacher, they addressed him as "Spank." Mostly, though, they made fun of his last name. They found many opportunities for humor in the name Oldham.

Surprisingly, Henry had not added such jesting to his list of annoyances. He believed that this was a legitimate field of kid humor, and sometimes teased his friends about their names.

Henry was impatient for school to end that day. Eventually, the bell rang and he headed for downtown. The address was a large, six-story office building. In the lobby, Henry had to go through a security checkpoint. He had to empty his many pockets and remove his belt. Then he went through a metal detector. As usual, Henry wondered why the fillings in his teeth didn't set off the alarm.

The office he wanted was on the fourth floor. The sign on the heavy glass door read: "D of T. Come in."

Henry entered and was greeted by a friendly looking older black man in a blue suit. The large I.D. badge hanging around his neck read: "Fred Tyler, D of T."

"You must be Mr. Henry Oldham," said Mr. Tyler. "You're right on time. I'm Frederick Tyler."

"Hello," said Henry, looking about the room, which was furnished with several metal office desks and filing cabinets. On one wall was a framed color photo of the President of the United States.

"Are you interested in recycling?" asked Mr. Tyler.

"Very much so," said Henry.

"Can you give me some examples of your experience in this field?" the man asked.

"I always recycle my father's newspapers. And our cans and bottles. When I'm walking about, I often find recyclables and put them in my pocket."

"You have many pockets," observed Mr. Tyler. "But how much can they really hold?"

"A great deal," said Henry, "because I modified one of them." Henry unzipped one of the pockets in his cargo pants, and folded out a large attached black nylon bag."

"Very resourceful," said Mr. Tyler. "Did you sew that yourself?"

"Yes, I did," said Henry. "Sewing isn't hard. You just move the needle tip back and forth, then pull it through the cloth. You have to be careful that you don't poke yourself."

The man was impressed. "Henry, I can see that you are a dedicated recycler. I believe you are just the sort of person we are looking for."

Henry appreciated the praise, but remembered to be on guard in case Mr. Tyler tried to sell him something.

Mr. Tyler walked over to a filing cabinet and removed a large brown paper bag from the bottom drawer. He put it down beside Henry.

"Henry, can you identify what's in this bag?"

Henry examined its contents. "It appears to be old torn and crumpled dollar bills."

"Exactly so," said Mr. Tyler. "After the government prints a fresh new dollar bill, it goes through many hands via your normal daily commerce. Eventually, it reaches this stage. Do you know what the government does with bills in this condition?"

"I believe they are shredded and recycled," answered Henry.

"Exactly so. Billions are shredded every year. But there's a problem with that."

"What sort of problem, sir?" asked Henry.

"Shredding all that money is very hard on the employees. They often get depressed. There's quite a high turnover of personnel in that department. So, the powers that be have decided to try something new. They've decided to divert a small part of that stream of discarded money to outside recyclers. Are you interested?"

Henry was definitely intrigued. "Yes, Mr. Tyler. What sort of work would be involved?"

"Every week I give you a bag of money. It's your job to recycle it."

"Recycle it how?" asked Henry.

"That's up to you," said Mr. Tyler. "You could spend it. You could bury it in a compost pile. You could chuck it down a gopher hole. Be creative. But you can't give it directly to anyone or tell anyone about it."

"Why not?" asked Henry.

"Because I don't want a mob scene outside my office. Discretion is the watchword for this project. That's why we are limiting it to dedicated recyclers. Are you the sort of person, Henry, who can keep a secret?"

"Yes, I am," stated Henry with conviction.

"I believe you are," said Mr. Tyler. "In fact if there's a child in this city who can keep a secret, I wouldn't be surprised if he's standing in front of me right now."

Henry appreciated that vote of confidence. One of the items at the top of his list of annoyances was adults who didn't believe what he said.

"But here's the thing, Henry," added Mr. Tyler. "You can't hoard it or save it. Every week that money has to disappear out of your hands."

"Can I tell my parents?" asked Henry.

"Sorry, you can't tell anyone. This operation requires absolute secrecy. The government isn't messing around here. The consequences for a leak could be extremely grave for the guilty party. Am I making myself clear on this point?"

"Very clear," agreed Henry.

"Are you in?" asked Mr. Tyler.

"I'm in," said Henry. "You can count on me."

Mr. Tyler got a stapler out of a drawer, and stapled closed the top of the bag of money.

"We don't want the wind picking up," he chuckled, "and blowing these bills all over the street."

"No, sir," agreed Henry.

Mr. Tyler told Henry he should return at the same time next week for another bag. Then he shook his hand and wished him: "Godspeed on your mission."

Henry thanked him and headed off with his bag of money. He knew recycling was the responsible thing to do, but he never imagined it could be this exciting.

* * *

Henry knew the best place to hide his bag of money. Not in the house, because his sister was a ceaseless explorer of closets and cupboards. Both she and Henry's mother were always on the prowl.

He decided to hide the bag in his father's old car, which had gone untouched since they rolled it into the garage three years before. In that time it had acquired a thick layer of dust and all the tires had gone flat.

Henry was disappointed at the lack of progress, but not surprised. His father's job and family took up most of his time. Plus, he enjoyed his two main hobbies: reading old magazines and listening to the late great jazz saxophonist Paul Desmond. In fact, if you were wrestle Henry to the ground and twist his arm, you might be able to get him to admit that his middle name was Desmond.

Henry hid the bag in the trunk of the car, then went in to see his mother. She asked him many questions about his job interview, but Henry's replies were terse and evasive. He said he had put in his application, and, no, the man had not tried to sell him anything.

"Did he offer you any snacks?" asked his mother.

"No, Mom, they were very businesslike. Can I go out and play now?"

"OK, but come in when you see your dad's car pull into the driveway. You know he doesn't like to wait for his dinner."

Henry got some transparent tape from his desk and went out to the garage. He flattened out the crumpled bills on the floor of the garage and repaired the badly torn ones with tape. He discovered that the bag contained 528 one-dollar bills. This was more money than Henry had ever seen before. Recycling it all before next Friday would take some careful thought and planning.

At dinner that night his father asked Henry more questions about his job interview. Once again he had very little to say beyond the fact that he had "put in his application." Henry didn't like to lie to his parents, so he decided the best tactic was to say as little as possible. Fortunately, both of his parents spent most of the meal trying to persuade Sally to eat something.

It seemed obvious to Henry that his sister was being difficult just to get attention. But he considered Sally to be his parents' project, and didn't comment or interfere. If he ever had any children, Henry expected that he would be sending away them to military school as soon as they learned to walk and talk. Then, when they had been trained in proper behavior, they could come home and rejoin the family.

After dinner, Henry helped his father do the dishes while his mother gave his sister a bath. As usual, Paul Desmond was playing on the stereo. Henry had heard all of his father's CDs a zillion times. He didn't really think about the music–it was just something that was there, like the pink roses on the kitchen wallpaper. Henry enjoyed making small talk with his father as he dried the dishes and put them away. It was something they did together every night, except when the family went out to dinner.

Henry knew that two children was a big drain on his father's income. He decided he would try to think of a way to give some of his recycled money to his father.

But how to do it? That was the problem! Serious brain work would be required.

The next day was Saturday, Henry's favorite day of the week. After breakfast, he went out to the garage and stuck a wad of money into his nylon wallet. His normally thin wallet had never bulged so fat. The Velcro flap could barely hold it closed. This would not do, Henry decided. He removed some of the bills, rolled them up, fastened them with a rubber band, and stuck them in a pocket. That's better, thought Henry–thankful again that his pants offered so many pockets.

Henry decided to recycle his first batch of money at a toy store downtown.

"How can I help you?" asked the tall bald man behind the counter.

"I'd like a squirt gun with a knob on the end that lets you rotate the nozzle in different directions," said Henry.

"Say what?" said the man.

Henry repeated his request. He pointed out that this highly desirable feature let you aim the gun in one direction while squirting some unsuspecting person in an entirely different direction.

"Such a thing exists?" asked the clerk.

"Of course," said Henry. "I read about it in a magazine."

"Hey, Dad!" called the clerk, "you ever hear of a squirt gun with a rotating nozzle?"

An elderly man shuffled out from a back room. "Yeah, but we haven't carried one of those in years. Not for decades in fact."

"Sorry, kid," said the clerk. "But squirt guns are passé. What you want is one of these water blasters. Check it out. You've got your massive two-quart water reservoir, twin-piston air pump, and you can blast a drenching stream over a distance of 50 feet."

"Not interested," sighed Henry.

Henry did spend $23 (including tax) on a deluxe yo-yo that was precision-machined of aircraft aluminum. He made sure to select one that was the same color red as his old wooden yo-yo. He was hoping his parents wouldn't notice the difference.

When he paid with his ragged bills, the clerk commented, "Where'd you get this money, kid? Did you raid your dead grandpa's wallet?"

"Both of my grandfathers are alive," Henry replied. "One lives in Pasadena and one in Florida."

"Glad to hear it," said the clerk. "You come back with that magazine article, and I'll see if I can order you the squirt gun."

"Thank you," said Henry.

On the walk home, Henry passed several markets, where he could have gone in and splurged on gobs of candy. But

Henry didn't want to rot out his teeth. He had spent several unpleasant hours in the dentist's chair and didn't care to repeat the experience. Besides, the only candy he really liked was the maple-walnut fudge they sold at the county fair. His practice was to eat a one-quarter pound wedge at the fair, then brush his teeth thoroughly when he got home. This once-a-year treat was enough to satisfy his candy cravings.

It took several minutes for Henry to locate the squirt-gun article. It was from *Popular Mechanix* of July, 1957. OK, Henry conceded, that was from quite a while ago. But he found it shocking that such a wonderful squirt gun was no longer being made. Clearly, some toy company was missing out on many millions in sales.

Sighing, Henry returned the magazine to the shelf. His father's bookcase contained hundreds of such magazines–all from a time long before Henry was born. His father loved to read test reports on 1952 DeSoto sedans and study how to build your own walkie-talkie powered by a single radio tube. Henry, to his father's surprise, found these articles just as fascinating. They had spent many a rainy afternoon absorbed together in the musty old magazines. People sometimes commented that in Henry's case the acorn hadn't fallen very far from the tree–whatever that meant.

That evening the family drove the dozen miles to the coast and ate dinner in a seafood restaurant. They got a table that looked out on the bay where several sea lions were swimming about. When he finished his salmon, Henry excused himself and went to the rest room. While there, he left a large roll of money on the floor behind the toilet.

* * *

Henry was impressed with his new yo-yo. It could "sleep" very nicely at the end of the string, then return smoothly at the slightest tug. He accomplished a challenging "around the world" maneuver on his very first try. Henry found it quite satisfying to operate such a precision device. He felt he had found the proper tool at last to enhance his skills. He would like to have shown it to his friends, but he knew it would be difficult to explain how he had obtained such an expensive toy. His friend Eddie, for example, might suspect that he had stolen it. Eddie himself had once been caught slipping a comic book down his shirt.

No, the yo-yo–like the bag of money–would have to remain Henry's secret.

That Sunday afternoon Henry went to the library. He located some of the books he had enjoyed over the years. He slipped dollar bills into the pages, then returned the books to the shelves. He felt that readers who shared his taste in authors deserved a reward. He managed to recycle over $75 this way without being spotted. Yes, Henry found that recycling money could be a very rewarding activity.

That week Henry left rolls of money in several more rest rooms. He visited laundromats and inserted dollar bills in the religious pamphlets left there for customers to read. He went to a city park and dropped a roll of money down a hole in an oak tree. By Thursday evening he had recycled all 528 dollar bills in his possession.

At lunch on Friday Henry told his mother he would be a few minutes late from school since he had some books to return to the library. This was not a lie, as Henry had checked out some books just for this purpose.

"No problem," said his mother. "And while you're downtown, why not check in about that recycling job?"

"Uhmm, that's a thought," muttered Henry.

When he went to the library after school, Henry was surprised to find it considerably more crowded than usual. People were removing books from shelves, fanning the pages, then moving on to the next book. It was almost as if they were searching for something.

Henry placed his books on the RETURNS counter, then left quickly. He walked around the corner, went through the security checkpoint, and took the elevator to the fourth floor. Mr. Tyler greeted him warmly.

"Ah, Henry, my chief recycler, it's good to see you."

"It's nice to see you again, Mr. Tyler."

"And how did your mission go, Henry?"

"Very well, sir. I recycled all my money."

"Good, Henry. But we don't use that term. We prefer to refer to the items in question as surplus scrap."

"Uh, right. I recycled all my surplus scrap."

"And did you tell anyone about it?"

"No, sir. I did not."

"Very good, Henry. I can see my faith in you has been justified. Are you ready for your next recycling mission?"

"Yes, sir."

"Good man." Mr. Tyler retrieved another brown paper bag from a filing cabinet. "We're moving you up to fives this week, Henry."

Henry inspected the bag. Sure enough, it was filled nearly to the brim with tattered and crumpled $5 bills.

"My, that's a lot of, uh, surplus scrap!" gasped Henry.

"Just think of it as tired old paper," said Mr. Tyler, stapling the top of the bag closed.

"You have a nice day. And I'll see you same time next week."

"Right, sir," said Henry, snapping off a brisk salute.

Mr. Tyler smiled and returned the salute.

As before, Henry flattened, repaired, and counted the scrap bills on the floor of the garage behind his father's old car. This time the bag contained 532 bills, making a total of $2,660.

Wow, thought Henry, that's enough to buy a battery-powered moped. Or even two!

Henry had long regarded a battery-powered moped as the ideal transportation system for a mechanically minded youth such as himself. But he knew his parents would insist he was "much too young." And if he acquired one with his surplus scrap, how would he explain such a purchase to his parents? No, the entire idea was impractical–even though Henry had spent countless hours imagining himself tooling about town on an efficient and practical two-wheeled machine. Bright yellow was Henry's preferred moped color, but he was also open to silver-blue.

"Rats," sighed Henry, wishing he were at least 16, independently wealthy, and very mature-looking for his age.

Saturday morning found Henry back in the city park with his pockets loaded with uncrisp $5 bills.

This time he was trying something new.

"Excuse me, ma'am," he said to an older woman, "I believe you dropped this."

The woman took Henry's offered bill. "Oh, did I? Thank you." She stuffed the $5 bill into her purse and hurried away.

Henry discovered that people who looked most in need of a cash windfall often refused the offered money. By contrast, well-dressed people nearly always took the cash; some didn't even bother to say thank you.

Henry offered $5 to an elderly man seated on a bench. "Thanks," said the man, taking the bill, "I was hoping you'd get around to me."

"What?" said Henry, startled.

"I've been watching you, kid. You're giving away money."

"No, I'm not."

"Right. My mistake. I can see now I dropped this five bucks. Silly me. Well, if you want to unload any more, I'm more than willing to accept it."

"Uh, why's that?" asked Henry.

"Because I'm old and I'm living on a meager pension. After I pay for my rent and my medicines, I don't have much left over for luxuries like food."

"That's terrible," said Henry.

"Well, some people have it worse," sighed the old man.

Henry had an idea. "I don't suppose you can keep a secret?"

"Kid, I'm still keeping secrets for people who've been dead for 50 years. What's on your mind?"

"I'm trying to think of a way to give some money to my father."

"You mean so he doesn't know it's from you?"

"Exactly," replied Henry.

"Hey, piece of cake. I could help you with that. How much are you thinking of giving him?"

"Uh, $2,000."

"A very generous gesture. And if I helped you, how much could you donate to my worthy cause?"

"Would $500 be enough?" asked Henry.

"$500 for me would be a very acceptable gesture. Very acceptable indeed."

"But you have to promise me you'll keep it a secret," said Henry.

"Kid, you have so come to the right place. You have these sums in cash?"

"Yes, in $5 bills."

"Right. Well, that makes for a bulky package. We'll have to do some laundering of your funds."

"My bills are old. I don't think they'll stand up to washing."

"Not to worry, kid. Can you meet me here in the park on Monday?"

"I could meet you after school. Say around 4:00?"

"Perfect. What we'll need from you is three rolls of bills: two with $1,000 and one with $500. Can you do that?"

"No problem," said Henry. "I'm very good at counting out money and compacting the stacks into rolls. I'll put each one into a different pocket."

"Good plan, kid. And I see you're well-equipped with pockets."

"My name is He–"

"Hey, no names, kid. This is strictly a business proposition between honorable strangers."

"OK," said Henry. "Whatever you say."

"By the way, kid. I'm a decent guy, but you really shouldn't go around talking to strangers."

"I don't normally," said Henry. "But you remind me of my grandfather–the one who lives in Pasadena. Except you're even older than he is."

"Thanks, kid. You know where you'll be when you get to be my age?"

"No, where?"

"Dead for 20 years."

"What?"

"That was a joke, kid. Now run along and don't hand out any more money. It's not a safe activity."

* * *

Sunday morning found Henry's father reading the newspaper while eating his eggs.

"Says here they've been finding money in the main library," he commented.

Henry looked down at his plate and poked his eggs with his fork.

"Finding money," said his mother, struggling to insert food into her daughter. "How so?"

"In books," replied her husband. "Mostly in the children's section, but also in science and engineering. Lucky patrons have been opening books and scoring dollar bills."

"Probably some nice literacy advocate," said Henry's mother, "trying to encourage people to read."

"Well, I'm all for it," said Henry's dad. "I'd like to find some money in unexpected places."

Henry perked up his ears. This was very good news!

"You could sell that wreck of car that's hogging the garage," suggested Henry's mother.

"That car is an investment," he replied. "It's growing more valuable every day."

"If you ask me," she replied, "the only thing it's growing is more decrepit. And more irritating."

"Hank, you borrow a lot of books from the library," noted his dad, changing the subject. "You ever find any money in them?"

"Not yet," admitted Henry. "But I'd like to. You're not going to sell that car are you?"

"Not a chance, Son. We're driving to your high-school graduation in it. The whole family! You'll be the envy of your peers."

"Not very likely," said Henry's mother. "Unless Henry flunks all his classes and graduates at age 35. The car might be ready by then."

Henry's father rustled his paper and turned to the sport section.

That afternoon Henry played baseball with his friends. He hit a triple, grounded out to shortstop, walked, struck out, and hit a long double, scoring two runs. His team won 4-2. Henry preferred to play third base, but in this league the players rotated positions every inning. After the game, the parents took the players out for pizza. Henry made two trips to the salad bar because the restaurant didn't offer non-gluten pizzas. Henry liked salad, but he liked pizza even more. His father suggested (nicely) to the manager that they think about expanding their pizza options.

As they were leaving, Henry slipped $5 onto the pile of bills left on the table as a tip for the waiter. He would have left more, but $2,500 was taking a big bite out of his remaining surplus scrap.

After school the next day Henry hurried to the park where he found the old man seated on the same bench.

"Hi, kid," he said. "Are we processing some money today?"

"Yes, we are."

"Good. I was a little worried the whole thing had been a delusional senior moment. Are you ready on your end?"

"All ready," replied, Henry, patting one of his bulging pockets.

"Good, let's go."

"Where are we going?" asked Henry.

"To the post office," replied the man. "Where else?"

The big downtown post office was one block over from the library. Henry and the man waited in line until it was their turn at the service window.

"How can I help you?" asked the postal clerk.

"I'd like two money orders, each for $1,000," replied the old man, nudging Henry.

Henry removed the first big roll from his pocket and put it on the counter. Then he extracted the other large roll and put it beside the first.

"I'll have to count this," said the clerk.

"Be my guest," replied the old man. "I'm retired. I've got all day."

The clerk removed the rubber band from one roll and began counting the $5 bills. "Don't you have any better bills than this?" he asked.

"Sorry," replied the man, winking at Henry. "I'm an old guy with old money. It's a package deal."

After several minutes, the clerk finished counting and

had his machine print out the two money orders. The old man also bought a pre-stamped envelope. He paid for the envelope and the money order fees from his own wallet. He thanked the clerk and led Henry over to a service table by the post office boxes.

"See, kid. I shrank all that bulky money down to two small slips of paper. Now what's your dad's name?"

"David Oldham," replied Henry.

"Oldham, how's that spelled?"

"Like old ham," replied Henry.

The old man chuckled as he wrote as he wrote David Oldham on the money orders. "I bet you get teased for that name, kid."

"It's been known to happen. Won't my dad wonder why he's getting money orders in the mail?"

"I thought of that, kid. Give me a sheet of paper."

Henry tore off a blank sheet from his spiral notebook.

"What we're going to do, kid, is send your dad an anonymous letter."

"Dear David," he wrote in shaky letters with an old fountain pen. "I'm sorry I cheated you all those years ago. It's been on my conscience ever since. I hope this small payment can make some amends for the wrong I did you."

"But what if nobody cheated my dad?" asked Henry.

"Well, human nature being what it is, if he's old enough to have a son your age, he's probably been cheated a few times by now. How should we sign it?"

"A friend?" suggested Henry.

"Nah, we'll sign it: Yours, Very Regretful."

"That's much better," agreed Henry.

The man folded the letter around the money orders, slipped them into the envelope, and sealed the flap. He wrote "David Oldham" on the envelope and then the rest of the address as Henry dictated it to him. Then he handed the envelope to Henry and watched as he slipped it into the outgoing mail slot.

"It should get there tomorrow, kid. I hope your dad doesn't drop dead of a heart attack when he opens it."

"I hope not too," said Henry.

The old man moved an arm behind his back. "Go behind me, kid," he whispered, "and drop the other roll into my hand."

Henry did as instructed. The man quickly transferred the roll of fives to an inside pocket of his shabby coat.

"I'm not leaving you short am I, kid?"

"Not at all. You did me a big favor. I can't thank you enough."

"Don't mention it, kid. Well, I think I'll go to the market and buy a whole strawberry pie. I really like strawberry pie!"

"I prefer banana-cream," said Henry, who was allowed to eat the filling but not the crust.

"Well, that's a valid choice too. Well, kid, if I see you around, remember: I don't know you and you don't know me."

"Right," said Henry. "And thanks again."

But the old man was already walking away.

* * *

Next day at school each minute crawled by like an hour for Henry. Finally, the bell rang and he ran all the way home as fast as he could. There on the hall table was the envelope and other mail waiting for Henry's dad. Since Henry was too distracted to do anything fun, he played with his sister Sally until his dad came home from work.

Fortunately, Henry's father enjoyed receiving mail. It didn't take him long to rip open the mystery envelope and read the surprising letter.

"Good gravy!" he exclaimed. "I'm rich!"

"What is it?" asked Henry's mother, startled.

"Somebody just sent me $2,000 in money orders! They claim it's repayment for cheating me years ago."

"Let me see that!" said Henry's mother, taking the letter and reading it.

"Oh, it's probably some scam," she scoffed.

"How can this be a scam?" demanded her husband. "Probably those money orders are counterfeit."

"Well, where's the profit in sending out fake money orders?" he demanded.

"Don't ask me," she replied. "But I bet it was mailed from some foreign country."

Henry's father examined the envelope. "No, it was mailed right here in town. We'll see if these money orders are fake. Hank, what time does the post office close?"

"Uh, 5:00, Dad."

Henry's father looked at his watch. "I've got 12 minutes. I can make it if I hurry. Honey, put the meatloaf on hold! I'm outta here!"

Henry's father had a triumphant grin on his face when he returned 45 minutes later.

"I'll have you know," he said to his wife. "Those were 100 percent genuine United States Postal Money Orders. They are legal tender for all debts public and private. You can spend them just like cash. In fact, the clerk I talked to had produced those money orders on his very own machine!"

"Well, who bought them?" she asked.

"Apparently, some ancient old guy accompanied by a kid, probably his grandson. My benefactor is some skinny senior citizen with a bad conscience."

"I know who it was," she replied. "It was the crook who sold you that car! No wonder he's riddled with guilt."

"I bought that car from a young guy. He had no idea what a valuable car he was selling. If anything, I should be the one feeling guilty."

Henry's mother uttered a sound suggesting great skepticism. "And what did you do with the money orders?" she asked.

"I stopped at the bank and deposited them."

"Good," she replied. "We're all overdue for our dental checkups. I'll make the appointments tomorrow."

Both Henry and his dad looked equally stricken.

"What!" exclaimed Henry's father. "You intend to use my legacy to pay the damn dentist?"

"Well, you're the one complaining about a sore tooth," she replied. "And the house insurance is due next week. This money will come in handy."

Henry's father looked at his son. "Well, Hank, it was a glorious dream while it lasted."

"Yes, Dad," sighed Henry. "It was."

The next morning when Henry's father opened his newspaper, eleven $5 bills fell out of it. The bills were old and some were taped.

"Holy cow!" he exclaimed. "More manna from heaven!"

"How did that money get in there?" asked Henry's mother.

"Probably a malfunction at the printing plant," replied Henry's dad, quickly gathering up the bills and putting them in his wallet.

"You intend to keep that money?" asked his wife.

"No, I'm giving it to the deserving poor: myself. Besides, I'll bet it's a promotion. Every week some lucky subscriber finds 55 bucks in his newspaper."

"If it's a promotion," replied his wife, "why haven't we heard about it?"

"I don't know, dear. Maybe it's a secret promotion. Newspapers are always trying something new to build circulation. I can use the money this weekend. Hank, you know what's on Sunday?"

"What, Dad?"

"The flea market!"

Henry's father loved flea markets nearly as much as he loved old magazines and Paul Desmond.

On Thursday after school Henry went to the dentist. He didn't have any cavities, but he had to endure some serious probing as the dentist scraped the tartar off his teeth. Henry got compliments from both the dentist and her assistant, but they weren't so pleased with Henry's sister. She set a new world's record for non-cooperation in the dentist's chair. Nor was Henry's father that agreeable as the drilling commenced into his bad tooth.

Twenty-four hours later, Henry was doing something much more fun: he was staring into a brown paper bag stuffed with $10 and $20 bills.

"Any problem handling this week's surplus scrap?" asked Mr. Tyler.

Henry gulped. "Not at all, Mr. Tyler. It will be a pleasure."

"Glad to hear it," said Mr. Tyler, stapling closed the bag. "We're starting to make a dent in our big recycling pile, thanks to you, Henry. You're doing a great job."

"I find it an exciting challenge," admitted Henry. "This is the best job I ever had!"

"Good," said Mr. Tyler. "A happy employee is a productive employee. Well, see you next week."

"See you then," said Henry, snapping off another salute.

Mr. Tyler returned both his salute and his wave.

As usual, Henry did his counting and currency repair work on the floor of the garage in the cobwebby dimness behind the old car. The bag contained 324 $10 bills and 278 $20 bills. The math was not much of a challenge for Henry, who was something of a wiz at multiplication. He found the total came to $8,800.

"Wow!" exclaimed Henry. "Wow and double wow!"

As before, he hid the money in the trunk of the car until he could think of a way to recycle it.

* * *

The flea market on Sunday was in the parking lot of the Veterans Center, across from the fairgrounds a couple of miles south of downtown. It was a monthly event put on by the veterans as a benefit for their nurses education fund. The parking lot was jammed with vendors selling used goods on portable tables and from the backs of pick-up trucks. The Oldhams went methodically up and down the aisles so that they didn't miss anything. Henry's mother pushed Sally in her stroller and tried to prevent her from grabbing things.

It didn't take long for Henry's father to spot a box of old magazines. He picked a magazine off the top of the pile and leafed through it.

"Well, would you look at that, Hank. It's a test-drive report on the 1954 Packard. Isn't that a handsome automobile?"

Henry agreed the car looked like a winner.

"How much?" asked Henry's dad, waving the magazine at the vendor.

"Two bucks each," he replied.

"Two buck each," repeated Henry's dad. "You must be expecting the Vanderbilts and the Rockefellers to be dropping by."

"Well, make me an offer," said the vendor.

"Fifteen bucks for the whole box," replied Henry's dad.

"Oh, Dave," said Henry's mother. "Don't you have enough magazines already?"

"Hey, I'm negotiating here, dear. The wife thinks I have enough magazines already," he pointed out to the vendor.

"I could go $20 for the whole box," he said.

"Sold!" said Henry's father, extracting four $5 bills from

his wallet. He dumped the box in the bottom of the folding two-wheeled cart that he always brought with him to flea markets. It was Henry's job to pull the cart.

Henry's mother found some clothes for Sally and a toy piano. Henry's dad scored a Paul Desmond CD that he didn't have. It was unscratched and only cost a dollar. Henry found a book called *The Complete Guide to Mopeds*, published in 1973. All the mopeds featured were gas-powered, but Henry knew he would enjoy reading about them just the same. The seller wanted $1 for the book, but Henry bargained down the price to 75 cents.

Afterwards, they went to a restaurant that specialized in steaks. Henry's father said he wanted to give his repaired tooth "a real workout" on a "choice T-bone." The place was fairly expensive, but Henry's mother said it was OK because the dentist bill hadn't been as high as she expected.

All during the meal, Henry's dad tried to think of elderly men who might have cheated him over the years.

"I knew some wily poker players in the Army," he said. "But they were all my age. Not that I ever lost that much."

"I should hope not," commented his wife.

"I know!" said Henry's father at last. "Maybe it was the minister who married us. He could be laboring under a very serious case of guilt."

Henry's mother knew he was joking, but she didn't find it that funny.

When they got home, Henry's dad put the box of magazines in the utility room that was just off the kitchen. His bookcase was completely full. He told Henry he was thinking of building some shelves in the utility room for "additional storage of vital magazines."

"You've read those magazines a million times," suggested his wife. "Why don't you get rid of some of them?"

Henry's father looked shocked. "The contents of these

periodicals are golden," he replied. "I learn something new every reading. Besides, they're educational for the lad."

"I don't see the point of filling Henry's mind with a lot of obsolete technology."

"Progress cannot be made, dear, without a thorough grounding in what came before. That is a scientific fact. And what's that awful noise?"

"It's Sally practicing on her piano," she replied.

"You gave a toy piano to a two-year-old? You must be insane!"

"Well, you saw me buy it."

"I thought you were going to turn it into a planter."

Henry's mother liked to plant African violets in unlikely objects, such as old typewriters and cameras, clocks with the gears removed, and Henry's first baby shoes.

While he was drying the dishes the following evening, Henry remarked, "Gee. I wonder how many magazines are in that box?"

"Probably at least two dozen," replied Henry's dad, scrubbing the meatloaf pan. "I scored a real coup on that deal."

"Some of them could be duplicates," suggested Henry. "We might have read them already."

A dark look passed over his father's face. "We'll check that box tonight, Hank. Right after I finish with this damn pan. I swear your mother must bake this stuff on with an acetylene torch."

Eventually, Henry's father finished with the pan, and Henry followed him into the utility room. Henry's dad began digging into the box and removing magazines.

"Haven't got this one," he said. "Nope, this one's new. What the heck is this? *Modern Bride!* How did that get in here? I tell you, those flea-market sellers are always trying to pull a fast one. It's bad enough when they sneak in *Golf Di-*

gest. The only thing more boring than playing golf is reading about it. Hey, what's this down at the bottom?"

Henry's father removed a small cardboard box. He undid the tape fastening the lid, lifted it off, and sat back stunned.

The box contained several very large rolls of money. One held $10 bills and the other $20 bills.

"Holy mother of Toledo!" exclaimed Henry's dad. "Do you see what I see, Hank?"

"I think so, Dad. It looks like money."

At that moment Henry's mother walked in to see what was going on.

"Dear me!" she exclaimed. "Where did you get all that money?"

"Right here in the box of magazines that you didn't want me to buy," said Henry's dad.

"It must belong to the seller," she replied. "He must have forgotten it was in the box. We'll have to try to locate him."

"There are thousands of dollars here, dear," replied Henry's dad. "No one could forget about a pile of cash this big. That seller didn't even know what he had!"

"What do you mean, David?" asked his wife, looking worried.

"I mean just what I said. I'll tell you what this is. This is some old codger's mad money stash. See, all the bills are real old."

"What's a mad money stash?" asked Henry.

"It's a rainy day fund," replied his father. "A chunk of cash in reserve—just for emergencies. You know, in case a fellow has to blow town in a hurry. But then the old guy passed away, and his family dumped his stuff without checking it. That seller probably bought this box at an estate sale for $2, and turned around and sold it to me for $20. He's already made his profit."

"We should try to find the rightful owner," insisted Henry's mother.

"Right," her husband replied. "We'll put an ad in the paper. Found: one large stash of money. Please call if you lost it."

"Well, at the very least we should turn it over to the police," she replied.

"The police?" said Henry's dad. "This has nothing to do with the police. This is a case of abandoned property being lawfully purchased. Am I right, Hank?"

"I think so, Dad."

"You're darn right, Son. It's like when you buy a painting in a thrift store and it turns out to be by some hotshot like Picasso. Nobody suggests handing the picture over to the cops. I claim salvage rights to this box of money. Salvage rights are recognized by international law. You could ask any lawyer. Here, Hank, help me count it. You start with the ten-spots and I'll deal with the twenties."

"David, I'm feeling very uncomfortable about this," said Henry's mother.

"Well, I'm uncomfortable too, dear," he replied. "It's a shock being thrust into sudden wealth. But don't worry, everything will be fine."

"I don't understand how all of a sudden you're coming into all this money," she said.

"It's kismet, darling," he replied. "At long last all the stars are lined up, and they're funneling money straight into my wallet. What I've tapped into here is a cosmic gusher of cash. Now, don't distract me. I'm trying to count."

Against her better judgment, Henry's mother helped count the money. The total came to an even $8,800.

"Isn't that splendid, Hank?" asked his father, sitting back and admiring his salvaged property. "Isn't that a splendid pile of cash?"

"It's very impressive, Dad," Henry conceded.

"I feel nervous having this much money in the house," said Henry's mother. "Someone could break in and murder us in our beds."

"No one's going to break in here," said Henry's dad. "I happen to be a veteran of the United States Army."

"I feel perfectly safe, Dad," said Henry.

"You know, Hank, in Japan 88 is considered a very lucky number. So we're fortunate that the total came to $8,800."

"Very fortunate, Dad," agreed Henry. "Plus, we got some great magazines too."

"That's right, Son. We have many hours of pleasant reading ahead of us. Here, dear, here's a *Modern Bride* from 1956 you might find interesting."

Henry's mother took the magazine and swatted her husband over the head with it. She did it playfully though and with a smile.

* * *

The next morning Henry's father took an hour off work and had the old car towed to his mechanic's shop. Surprisingly, there wasn't that much wrong with it. It had stopped running because a wire was detached from the distributor. The mechanic changed all the fluids, belts, and hoses, and redid the brakes. He gave the engine a tune-up and installed a new battery.

When Henry's dad picked up the car, he drove straight to a tire store that was having a sale. He bought four new tires and got a fifth tire (for the spare) for free. He also negotiated an extra discount for paying cash.

Next, Henry's dad took the car to an auto upholstery shop. He instructed them to redo the interior in contrasting shades of yellow and green. He said he wanted a first-class job at a very reasonable price. The owner of the shop said he would give him a good deal and promised the job would be finished in about a week.

Riding the elevator up to his place of employment on Friday, Henry was worried that he would have to find a new place to stash his recyclables. He also wondered how he would cope this week if they moved him up to $50 bills. Or even $100 bills!

But when he entered the office, he was surprised to see that Mr. Tyler wasn't there. Instead, sitting behind the desk was a heavy-set man who looked like he needed to shave several times a day.

"Yes, what is it?" asked the man. His manner was very gruff.

"I'm here to see Mr. Tyler," replied Henry.

"Fred Tyler was transferred to Kansas. What's on your mind, junior?"

"Uh, I'm here to pick up this week's surplus scrap."

"All recycling programs with outside contractors have been terminated," said the man.

"Oh," said Henry. "Really?"

"That is the case. Now move along, sonny. This is a busy office."

"Will Mr. Tyler be back next week?"

"I suggest you forget about Mr. Tyler. And the entire program. Of course, you're still sworn to secrecy."

"I understand," said Henry. "OK."

"Don't let the door slam on your way out."

Riding back down in the elevator, Henry was disappointed but not surprised. All in all, the job had seemed too good to be true.

When he got home, Henry told his mother that he had checked on the recycling job. He told her they had hired someone else, but were keeping his application on file.

"Oh, they always say that, Henry. I wouldn't get your hopes up. They probably wanted someone older."

"Right, Mom. That's what I thought too."

The upholstery shop did a wonderful job on the new interior. Henry found it hard to believe it was the same car. He and his dad spent a long weekend working on the car. They removed the bumpers, grille, lights, and all the chrome trim. Then they sanded every inch of the body with fine-grit sandpaper that they dipped frequently in water.

The next day, Henry's father took another hour off work to drive his car to an auto paint shop. Originally, the car had been painted a meek pale yellow. But Henry's dad wanted a deluxe two-tone paint job. He specified a sunny lemon-yellow for the top half and a bright lime-green for the bottom half.

Several days later, when Henry's father came home with the repainted car, he drove it straight into the garage before anyone could see it. He said the garage was "off limits" for at least two weeks while the new paint was hardening. Henry wanted to peek into the garage, but he was good at resisting such impulses. He knew his father wanted the car to be a surprise.

At last, the two weeks came to an end. One Saturday morning in June, Henry's dad opened the garage doors and drove the car out into the driveway. Everyone was amazed by the transformation. The restored car was a gleaming beauty!

Henry and his dad spent the rest of the day reattaching the bumpers, grille, lights, and chrome trim. When the car was finished, many of the neighbors walked over to admire it. Henry's father said they could look, but warned them not to touch anything. He did leave one door open so they could inspect the matching interior.

The next day the Oldham family went for a long drive in their sharp yellow and green car. Many passing drivers honked and waved when they saw the beautiful car. Even Henry's mother had several complimentary things to say about it. Fortunately, the shiny new vinyl upholstery was washable, so Henry's father didn't get too upset when Sally threw up in the back seat.

Since Henry's father was so good at bargaining for discounts, he had only spent about half of his cosmic cash. The rest Henry's mother put into their savings account. She was beginning to suspect that Sally might need braces on her teeth someday.

Henry thought that riding with his dad in their restored car was one of the high points of that summer. He was proud that he had contributed in several ways to the project.

Henry saw the old man only one time after that. The man was sitting at an outdoor cafe and eating a piece of strawberry pie. The man saw Henry, winked, then looked away.

Years later, when Henry was 16, he built an electric-powered moped. He painted it a bright yellow and covered the seat with green vinyl. The moped had a top speed of 18 mph and could go about 30 miles (depending on hills) on each charge. Henry installed a solar panel on the roof of the garage to recharge his moped's battery. He buzzed back and forth to high school on the free energy provided by the sun. Henry was well known at his school for riding the moped and for always wearing zip-off cargo pants.

Many parts of the moped Henry had recycled from other uses. Everyone agreed that his pollution-free bike was an ingenious and creative demonstration of recycling.

But then that shouldn't have come as a surprise. Henry was always very good at recycling.

Made in the USA
Lexington, KY
24 October 2016